About the author

Meet Tony and Marsha Woods.

After a forty-year career as missionaries, Tony and Marsha have settled Down Under to be near kids and grandkids. "Life is a journey," they insist, and their travels have taken them to ministries in three African countries, Hong Kong, Thailand and Australia. Most of their time, however, was spent in Japan, where they raised three children and buried one.

Many of their books reflect life on the trail. In *River Crossings*, Marsha provides a personal glimpse of a missionary wife and mother. *Looking for a Lamb* chronicles the death of their firstborn son to leukemia. In *Anagaion* (Greek for *Upper Room*), new Christians and seekers are shown the essentials of faith, and in *Weaving Sunlight*, Marsha and Tony tie all of that and more together into a beautiful tapestry of two lives lived for Him.

This is a work of fiction. Names, characters, businesses, places, events and incidents are either the products of the author's imagination or used in a fictitious manner. Any resemblance to actual persons, living or dead, or actual events is purely coincidental.

Source of Bible references: The Holy Bible, New International Version, Copyright 1973, 1978, 1984 by International Bible Society. Broadman and Holman Publishers, Nashville, Tennessee

REACHING THE HEIGHTS
THE TRAIL ABOVE

TONY WOODS

REACHING THE HEIGHTS
The Trail Above

Vanguard Press

VANGUARD PAPERBACK

© Copyright 2022
Tony Woods

The right of Tony Woods to be identified as author of
this work has been asserted by him in accordance with the
Copyright, Designs and Patents Act 1988.

All Rights Reserved

No reproduction, copy or transmission of this publication
may be made without written permission.
No paragraph of this publication may be reproduced,
copied or transmitted save with the written permission of the
publisher, or in accordance with the provisions
of the Copyright Act 1956 (as amended).

Any person who commits any unauthorised act in relation to
this publication may be liable to criminal
prosecution and civil claims for damages.

A CIP catalogue record for this title is
available from the British Library.

ISBN 978 1 80016 377 5

*Vanguard Press is an imprint of
Pegasus Elliot Mackenzie Publishers Ltd.*
www.pegasuspublishers.com

First Published in 2022

**Vanguard Press
Sheraton House Castle Park
Cambridge England**

Printed & Bound in Great Britain

Dedication

We would like to dedicate this book to our son, Trevor. He was the first to fall, a victim of leukemia most likely acquired while we were in Zambia. The enemy of this world was quick to take credit, but we rest in the assurance that only God has the final Word on these things. We look forward to our own 'final words' as we enter His Kingdom, which I'm convinced will be something like, "Thank you, Lord, for that valley You led us through. And thank you for the assurance that Trevor will be waiting to welcome us."

What stories we'll have to share with you, Son! And I believe you'll be delighted to see all the wonderful things that came about through our shared grief at losing you. It's been a great journey; see you soon.

Foreword

While this book was written in a matter of weeks, the making of it has taken seventy-four years so far. I was aware of the journey, at least from a child's perspective, when I gave my life to Jesus at the age of nine. The perception of it was more pronounced ten years later. My wife was praying for me from her own dorm room in another university over a thousand miles away. She and her roommate, Pattie, had decided that it was time to pull out the big guns.

Marsha had committed her life to a mission-centered ministry several years before, but even then, her wisdom told her that to make such a decision public could change a young man's career plans for all the wrong reasons. The last thing she wanted was for some boy to 'get the call' to missions in order to be considered as marriage material. So, she kept her cards close, casually sizing up the line of suitors that inevitably made their way to her doorstep. I was only one of a series who was vying for Marsha's affections, and felt privileged when I got the chance to take her out on a date.

The evening progressed and the talk came around to future plans She looked up into the sky and said, "So, what are you planning to do after you graduate?"

Trying to find the particular star to which she was devoting so much of her attention, I answered, "Well, after two years in forestry, I've decided that's not for me. I'm told that the only other course credits I have are in English, so I guess I'll look into teaching."

There was a visible slump in her shoulders, and I was sure I could hear the sound of air escaping as from a balloon. She didn't comment, but our relationship from that point had grown decidedly icy. It wasn't until later I discovered that I had just been scratched off her short list.

I tried for another year to gain her favor; at one point I even asked her outright why we couldn't consider going to the 'next level', whatever that meant. She answered that question for me when she said in a completely straight face, "I could never marry a Texan."

I didn't see that one coming. "Why not?" I asked.

"They're just too proud."

I tried to explain to her that, while Texas was a unique state, and that people from there often excelled, I was in no way proud of the fact. Wrong answer.

The following year, Marsha graduated from high school and moved to Omaha, Nebraska to attend the same Christian university that many of her friends had entered. Close proximity resulted in clearer vision, and Marsha began to see that 'Christian life' could be quite attractive on the outside, but something entirely different on the inside. Some of the boys, she discovered, were at the end of the day simply 'some of the boys' and unworthy of the calling they professed. Her short list just about exhausted, she and her friend Pattie looked back over to rejected applicants.

"What about Tony?" Pattie suggested, and I can imagine Marsha thinking to herself, *Yeah, what* about *that handsome hunk of a man with his dreamy eyes and divine smile?* She denies any such thoughts, but a guy can aspire.

The two girls decided to pray, and their prayers were heard. At that very moment, over a thousand miles away, I was studying for a chemistry test. Looking through the textbook, I tried to anticipate what questions might come up on the exam. 'What are the properties of a filtrate?' Check. 'What is the equation for salt?' Check. 'Why not go into full time Christian ministry?' What?

Where did *that* come from? I looked back through the book, but found nothing to suggest such a question. Finally, for the first time in my life, I got on my knees, looked up at the ceiling, and said in a half whisper, "God? Was that You?" The peace that swept over me at that moment is something I will never forget, and something that has continued to sustain me through every valley and mountaintop.

The next day, I wrote a letter to Marsha. Remember, these were the days before email. I can't even remember now how it was that I had her address, since she had already told me I was yesterday's news. In my best hand-written script, I wrote, 'Guess what? I'm going into full time ministry!'

You might think she would be surprised and happy at my decision, but the cynic in her was convinced that Pattie had told me her secret. The letter I got back a week later was smoking. 'If you want to do something stupid like that, I guess it's your business.'

I was stunned, unable to imagine what button I had inadvertently pushed. I wrote back and said something to the effect, 'I can't understand why the first thing that would happen is that God would take away the one person I love. But this thing is real. So goodbye, I guess.'

Marsha called me from a pay phone, and says she'll never forget the sound of quarters dropping through the slot. She got right to the point. "Did Pattie tell you?"

"Tell me what?" I asked, trying to keep the fear out of my voice.

"That I've been planning to marry a missionary!"

"Uh… No."

We were married eight months later, and the journey has led us to ministries in three African countries, Thailand, Hong Kong, Australia (where we eventually retired), and Japan, where we spent most of our forty-year career, and where we raised three kids and buried one.

And that's what this book is about: the journey. In the pages to follow, you'll read about a man and his wife on a backpack trip. You'll meet challenges, loneliness, fear, grief and friendships that can be found nowhere else. And you'll follow this couple to the summit of a mountain where only one will come back down. If you want a more detailed account of the journey, I'd invite you to look at our memoirs, *Weaving Sunlight*. But what I want to accomplish here is to take you on your own personal journey. I can almost guarantee that the things the pilgrim experiences are the kinds of things that anyone who follows the path set before them by God will experience. And I don't want you to just experience them; I want you to learn from them and thrive as a child of God.

Death is the last challenge facing every pilgrim, and so far, I can't write from a personal experience. For us, it seems, we are only appointed once to die, so that's a one-time experience. Until then, however, coming face to face with one's mortality is a pretty good substitute. As missionaries these past forty years, Marsha and I have come very close more than once to meeting our Maker. Marsha drew so near back in Liberia, she says that, "It was like crawling up to the edge and looking down."

But those experiences have only brought comfort, and a strength to face the unknown that we might not have found otherwise. Recently I was diagnosed with a particularly virulent form of cancer, "aggressive and broken out" as the doctor explained it. It's being treated, and as of today, I have every reason to believe that we'll lick this one. But I have no illusions. There will come a time, I'm sure, when I'll hear the words of my Savior, and He'll be saying something like, "Hey Tony, do you want to see something really cool? C'mon up!"

Until then, I hope I can encourage my fellow pilgrims to take heart. We're never alone, and we can't lose. Let's get started.

Episode One
The Day Begins

The mountaintops lining the horizon of the eastern sky had a vague glow about them, in contrast to those in the west that seemed to grow darker by the moment. Birds in the valley below expressed their anticipation in an ever-growing chorus of worship unlike anything man could ever duplicate.

The glowing line was moving in almost imperceptible degrees, its intensity diminishing along either end while increasing at one point near the center of his vision. Then suddenly, the point changed from indistinct glow to blazing light, its rays bursting in all directions as it vanquished the darkness crouching in the lowest part of the valley.

The man known by fellow travelers only as Friend took another sip of his coffee, smiled at the growing light show and whispered, "Thank you." He had been on this journey for more years than he cared to admit, the decision made as a young man so long ago. He still remembered that day as clearly as yesterday, even without opening up his journal and reading.

Come, he had written. *Come out of the darkness and into the light. Come to Me, and learn what real life is all about.* With those words, the invitation found its way into my heart, and my heart was ready. My days had been filled with a constant barrage of things that battled for first place, and I had fallen, the first victim. The only thing left was unconditional surrender to God; and what followed was a sense of unconditional love, and a peace that I never thought possible. It was a feeling I knew I could never understand, not fully. Small wonder, then, that those closest to me were unable to grasp it either. My friends, my associates, even my own family were left mystified at the change. I pray every day for their acceptance, but my longing is tempered by an overwhelming desire to know Him better. He had said, *Come*. I came, and now nothing else really matters.

'But His next word following *come* only served to increase my ignorance. He said, *Go. Follow the path that I have set before you. Learn all you can about the path, because it is in the journey that you will find Me.*

'Come. Go. Learn. Strange words indeed. Strange, perhaps, but not difficult to understand, nor to obey. I must go and observe all that I am shown. His Word I will carry with me, and each day I will record what I see. I don't know where the journey will end; How long is a lifetime? But I do know that it could come to a close at any point along the way. I'm not to worry about what I can't see, but only to see what I am shown, and in the process to become more and more what I've been created to be. I can't wait to begin.'

Friend smiled to himself as he took another sip of coffee. Yeah, easy words to say, he thought. Even putting them on paper was not a great challenge. But the *living* of those words… oh the living! First there was the loneliness. Those closest to him tried but just couldn't bring themselves to accept his decision to take the journey. They questioned, they cajoled; in moments of frustration, they openly condemned his actions. What nonsense! they insisted. How can you put aside all that you've worked for, all that… well, all that has made you what you *are*? And for what? An invisible Power that you say has called you to a journey with no parameters, except that you are to stay to the trail, keep moving forward and learn from what you experience along the way.

Even his own family could not accept it. His daughter might have, but she was too young to grasp such things. Her older brother wanted to believe; this was his father, after all. But in all the uncertainty, he chose to remain behind, doing what he could to keep peace in the family, often sticking up for his dad, pleading with his mother to try and understand.

And she did try; Lord knows, she wanted to follow her husband on this journey of faith. But the faith just wouldn't come and she drew back in fear mingled with confusion. The days turned into weeks and he persisted in his pilgrimage. In reality, he never left home, but he became a stranger, an oddity among his peers and an object of ridicule at work. More and more, it seemed, he was alone in a world that no one around him could share. But even as those dearest to him were drawing away, the world he had entered became more and more real, the experiences more filled with hope and assurance until he became convinced that the journey would provide the only hope, not just for his own survival but for his whole family.

Think about this:

Can you identify with the feeling of isolation even among friends and family as a result of a particular stand you've taken? Has your decision placed you in a whole new world, where even your closest friends and family cannot enter? The life of faith has often been described in those terms, and the way it plays out in day-to-day living cannot be underestimated.

This fact is crucial to fully understanding the pages that follow. *Reaching the Heights*, at one level, is simply the story of a man on a backpack trip. Looking closer, several logistical questions emerge: where is he buying his food? Where is his family? Where can he travel for a lifetime through a wilderness such as he describes?

This is where the reader's imagination comes into play. The stories are presented in realistic terms, but they are in fact an allegory. When the pilgrim made his decision to follow God's will, he was immediately confronted on every side by those who could not understand. With each step into the journey, he found himself further and further removed from the world of those around him. This book focuses on that new world, complete with unique friends, new commitments and heretofore unknown dangers. It is quite possible that you, the reader, can identify with these surroundings. The pilgrim's name is not revealed, in the hope that anyone can identify with him. The choice of gender is based mainly on the fact that I can explore best from my own perspective, but it is hoped that any reader can experience the pilgrim's journey regardless of persuasion.

Pray today for clarity, as you examine your world. Pray for wisdom and courage; ask God to show you His will for your life. Then when that understanding comes, step out in the assurance of His Presence!

And when you turn to the right or when you turn to the left, your ears shall hear a word behind you, saying, "This is the way; walk in it."

Isaiah 30:21

Episode Two
An Old Friend

The lifetime commitment to follow his Master was underscored time and again on the trail through the people Friend met and the challenges he encountered. In a world where names more often than not reflected one's identity, the pilgrim became known only as 'Friend'. Old Charlie was the first to introduce him to others in that way, and before long it was just easier to let himself be known as a friend to all. Charlie (whose 'Old' designation helped define him) took him under his care and helped him understand more and more the depth of his commitment, sharing in his gentle easy-going way what it meant to be on this journey. Daily difficulties were made easier with the understanding that the trail was leading to something. *Someone* more wonderful than he could ever have imagined. Even in times of great pain and suffering, Friend was able to draw strength from his growing faith, knowing that he was perfectly loved by the very One Who created him.

The understanding was sharpened and made stronger thanks to Charlie's leading him to the place called Rendezvous. Here was a gathering of fellow pilgrims who met together regularly along the trail, enjoying a fellowship like Friend had never known before. They prayed together, sang together, worshipped together. Those with more experience offered training in the ways of the journey. Every day at Rendezvous was a cacophony of sounds: laughter, tears, music, even of warfare as skills were honed that would help the pilgrims in times of spiritual attack. Then the camp would break up and everyone would resume the journey, anticipating the next time they could come together.

Weeks became months, the months stretched into years, and still Friend continued toward the goal. Along the way, he suffered loneliness, hunger, sickness and discouragement. But looking back, he could also see the Hand of God bringing him through every circumstance, emerging stronger than before. With the growing strength came a growing responsibility to help those younger in the faith, and Friend was eager to reach out to them. Eventually, he was chosen to lead Rendezvous, helping to break camp, move to the next location and set up, then prepare the programs that would benefit all who came into the fellowship. One of the most eager newcomers was his own son, who showed up one day and joined the pilgrims. His mother and sister were doing well, he was told, and perhaps coming to faith… but not yet.

The days that followed were among the most joyful times Friend had ever experienced. His son was becoming a strong young man, so adept at everything.

Then one day, an angel appeared and told Friend, "Your son has been called to the mountaintop. You may go with him to the summit, but you will come down alone."

The mountain had been a constant presence along the trail, always in view no matter where the trail led him. He had known that it was a special place, open only by invitation. As father and son struggled up the slopes, they were met by a succession of lambs, each one offering an alternative to the summit. Thinking back over that time, Friend gave each lamb a name in keeping with the nature of the alternative. There was Anger, who reminded Friend of the injustice to which he was being subjected. Fight back, he was told. Don't let *Him* tell you what to do. Then there was Denial, who urged them to simply turn around and go back. When they moved on upward, they were met by the Warrior lamb. He was not alone, Friend was told. There were others who would defend his cause and bring both father and son back down the mountain safely. Join us, and live. Around the next bend, they met the lamb of Trade. Everything has a price, he said. I can fulfill your deepest desires; just agree to my terms.

They moved on, and met the Scapegoat, who incredibly offered himself to take the place of Friend's son. He would bear the burden, accept the knife and free the two to return back the way they had come. Friend had almost succumbed to the Scapegoat, until he realized that the deceiving lamb had no intention of making good on his promise, but only sought to convince them that obedience to *Him* was always optional.

The Magician's lamb demonstrated the enemy's desperation. Yes, there is a power beyond yourself, he told Friend. But *His* is not the only power. Join us, and we can build a new world free of His unfair demands. When that failed to deter, and the summit loomed nearer, out of the darkness came the Demon lamb, visible only by two yellow eyes that stood a head taller than Friend. "Back off!" the demon demanded. "You're into things you know nothing about. I have the power to kill and to spare. Choose wisely."

But desperation drove Friend to a new level of rage. Picking up a rock, he rushed headlong at the source of the evil eyes, only to be thrown to his back writhing in pain. At that point, the skies were opened, and the light revealed the demon to be nothing more than a small helpless creature resting on the ledge of a rock wall above them. The light also revealed all the lambs along the way for what they really were: attempts at deception on the part of an enemy who wanted nothing less than the soul of man.

The revelation enabled father and son to continue on to the top, where they met the Lamb of Lambs. In His eyes, they saw Truth for the first time on the ascent. Truth… and Love. There, the son parted company with the father, and was taken into a glorious light, leaving Friend with inexplicable joy at what he had seen, but also the unanswerable question that burned in his soul:

how was he ever going to come down from the mountain alive?

He did eventually make it down, but in the process lost the path, entering instead into a dreadful swamp filled with every horror imaginable. For days he languished, caring not whether he lived or died but wanting only to be taken from the exquisite pain that was ripping him apart. It was only through the help of a fellow pilgrim who called himself Pastor McAllen that he was finally able to return to the trail and begin the healing process. Healing did come, along with new purpose and new opportunities. Then there was that unforgettable day when his precious wife and daughter joined him. They traveled together, sharing the load of responsibility and growing more each day into what they had been created to be.

His daughter grew into a beautiful young woman, met a handsome young man, and now the two of them traveled together finding new dimensions of the journey that even Friend had not experienced.

A sound behind him interrupted Friend's musings. He turned and was met by the sight of Jake: caretaker of the trail, guide when needed, messenger, true friend and angel. "Jake! It's so good to see you. It's been… well… *years*!"

Think about this:

Can you identify with the 'lambs' Friend experienced on the way up the mountain with his son? They should be familiar to you, since the enemy uses them often, in his efforts to make you turn back from the journey you're on. Look at each one again, preferably with a loved one. See if you can track their actions in your own life or in the lives of those around you. Then prepare yourself for battle!

For our struggle is not against enemies of blood and flesh, but against the rulers, against the authorities, against the cosmic powers of this present darkness, against the spiritual forces of evil in the heavenly places. Therefore, take up the whole armor of God, so that you may be able to withstand on that evil day, and having done everything, to stand firm.
Ephesians 6:12–13

Episode Three
At the Campsite

Seeing the angel known simply as Jake, Friend was brought quickly to his feet. "Jake!" he called out. "It's so good to see you. It's been... well... years!"

Jake's smile crinkled into a grin, much as it would appear on an old but fit man. He had explained long ago that his appearance was God's mercy on those who moved along the trail. Revealing himself as he might have to those off the path could result in some "rather terrifying situations," Jake had explained. But on more than one occasion, this Heavenly Being had come to Friend with a word or two of encouragement. But... why *now*? he wondered.

As if reading his mind, Jake spoke softly. "You've traveled well, Friend. Through fires, floods and droughts, you've been faithful. Many travelers today look to you as teacher and mentor. You've got nothing to be ashamed of, and everything to rejoice about." Jake paused a moment to let that soak in, then continued, "And that's why I'm here this morning. I have a message for you. The mountain waits."

***

With two more cups of coffee in one hand, Friend pulled down the zipper on the tent door. To his left, he could just make out the form of his wife in the sleeping bag. She began to stir, then rolled over to face him. "Is that coffee I smell? Oh, sweetheart, you spoil me."

"Nothing's too good for the Bride of my Youth," Friend whispered, handing her the coffee cup, handle first. "How did you sleep?"

"Like a baby. I really like this campsite. The sounds of the river down in the valley are just like lullabies." She took a sip, then looked up at her husband. "I thought I heard you talking to someone. Do we have company?"

"Not any more. It was a short visit." He hesitated, then continued. "From Jake."

"Jake! The angel? I haven't seen him since, well, since we started the journey together and I was still trying to put the pieces together after—"

"Our son. That was quite a valley, all right. I don't know how we would have gotten through it without Jake's words of encouragement."

"So. Did Jake have some words of encouragement this time? Why show up now? And why wasn't I allowed to see him?"

Friend took a sip of coffee, which had now grown cold. "Let me see if I can put this together the way he did. He started by saying that I've been walking a good walk. I have — how did he put it? — *nothing to be ashamed of and everything to rejoice about*."

"That's good to hear. Of course, I knew that all along. You're a good man. Always have been. Always will be. But there was more, right?"

"Yeah. He said that it was time for me to head up the mountain."

"The mountain? But, what… why… I thought…"

Friend looked deep into his now empty coffee cup as if searching for words. Finding none, he looked directly into his wife's eyes. Understanding came like a bucket of ice water.

"Oh. No. No, no, no, no, no. That's not right. There's some mistake. Are you sure?"

"Jake never lies. And he never minces words. He had a message to deliver, and he delivered it. That's what he does, you know."

The cup in her hands had been forgotten, and was now spilling coffee all over the sleeping bag. Friend reached down gently and took it. "He also said that I'm supposed to go alone."

She hung her head as low as it would go, and huge tears began dropping from her nose to join the spilled coffee. "But *why?* Why can't I go with you? You got to go with our son. I should be able to go with you."

"I don't know, babe. I wish like everything you could come along, but maybe this is for the best. God does know what He's doing, after all.

"So when do you have to go?"

"Today. Right away. I'd like you to stay here in camp. It *is* a great site, after all," he smiled. "There'll be some people from Rendezvous passing by soon — maybe today or tomorrow at the latest. Join up with them and help them set up the next camp. You'll be a big help to them, and they'll provide whatever you need."

For the next little while, they cried together, prayed together, and finally began making plans. She prepared some simple meals to put into his pack that wouldn't require making a fire. He went through both packs, deciding together what he should take and what could be left behind. Reaching into one pocket, Friend pulled out a lion's tooth on a leather lace. "Here's something I think you should hold on to," he said, placing it in her hand. "It's a great reminder that the enemy has no power over us. Ever."

Years ago, and over a period of several months, the lion had been after Friend. He almost got the best of him one night, but his son had come through in the nick of time and killed the beast, using the sword Friend now carried everywhere. "I think you should have this, too," he said, handing her the blade.

"I wouldn't know the first thing about that," she said, refusing to touch it.

"Maybe not now. But there will be people at Rendezvous who do, and they can teach you the basics. At least give it a try, okay?"

She nodded and took the sword, her hands shaking as she tested its weight. "I just wish... I just wish we didn't have to think about things like this."

"I'm with you, babe. But the years have taught me that the enemy is never far away. And he's good at finding weaknesses. Make sure you don't show him any. And if the time comes when you have to use it, know that God will give you the strength you need, when you need it."

"I need strength right now," she said, her voice quavering. "Not for some overgrown cat, and not for some dumb demonic warrior we've seen around here. I need the strength to get on my feet and put one foot in front of the other."

"And that's exactly what we're promised," Friend said, taking both her hands into his. Remember Isaiah 40:31? *But those who wait for the LORD shall renew their strength, they shall mount up with wings like eagles, they shall run and not be weary, they shall walk and not faint.*

"That's what we both need right now, isn't it? Not the speed of a leopard nor the wings of an eagle; just the strength to move forward, one step at a time. And we'll do that, because it's been promised that we can. You can. I can."

One last time, they held each other in their arms and prayed. The angel Jake stood off a little way from the camp, unseen by both of them. He shared their sadness, but knew the joy that was coming. The enemy was not far away, hoping to take advantage of their grief. But they would not be coming any closer. Not today. Not while Jake stood there. And as they prayed, the strength did come. And at least they were able to smile through their tears and wave at each other while Friend made his way up the trail, toward the mountain.

Think about this:

What mountains loom over you today? Are their challenges that you're not sure you can handle? Anyone who faces an uncertain future is like that pilgrim, looking up, looking back, and asking, "Why? Why must I do this?" There is no single answer that will suffice for all of us, but there is a single hope. Jesus Christ knows what you are facing and He assures you that you are never alone. He will go with you every step of the way, and if you're a child of God, the end of the journey will bring peace, healing and a joy that we can't even imagine. When the enemy seems to surround you on all sides, look to the One Who holds all things, and Who holds you secure in His arms.

For I am convinced that neither death, nor life, nor angels, nor rulers, nor things present, nor things to come, nor powers, nor height, nor depth, nor anything else in all creation, will be able to separate us from the love of God in Christ Jesus our Lord.
Romans 8:38–39

Episode Four
Powers and Principalities Council

The room was filled with representatives from every level of oppression available to the Evil Man. At the bottom of the scale were the 'cannon fodder': those ugly brutes whose job it was to terrify and when possible, to take out pilgrims along the trail. They were vaguely man-like in appearance but unlike any man the world had seen. Bulging muscles, grey reptilian skin and a huge club were usually the only things remembered by people who had the misfortune to come face to face with one and lived to tell the tale. While they obviously wanted to be part of this 'powers and principalities' council, about all they could manage was to grunt and snort while bashing their clubs on the ground.

A level or two above them sat the demonic chamchas, the nuisance specialists credited with everything from random headaches to stubbed toes inflicted on anyone who attempted a closer walk with their Creator. Taken individually, they rarely had much effect on faithful pilgrims who simply swatted them away with the Name of Jesus. Working together, however, they could succeed in tearing a person down, much like a persistent rash or an unrelenting Pekinese.

Many were the victims of these mischievous yet potentially deadly demons, most notably the man known only as Legion, possessed by more than could be counted and driven to insanity until he was rescued by none other than the Son of God Himself. Begging not to be thrown into the Abyss, a 'holding cell' where demons are kept for later judgment, they were instead allowed to inhabit a herd of pigs, who promptly threw themselves over a cliff rather than endure their agonizing harassment.

Watching the chamchas in quiet amusement were the deceivers. By their appearance, one would not think these principalities were much of a threat, but that in itself was reason enough to fear them. Their strengths were deception, after all. More often than not, they would reveal themselves to their potential victims as allies, ready and willing to help them out of difficult situations. The work of the deceivers usually came in a series of steps, each one drawing the believer further from his faith and closer to the enemy. The process was illustrated in Psalms 1:1, where it is written, *Blessed is the man who does not walk in the counsel of the wicked or stand in the way of sinners or sit in the seat of mockers.* The picture is of a hapless victim, walking by, then stopping to listen, and by the end of the day sitting with those who will bring him to ruin.

Seated at the highest echelon of attendees was the Evil Man himself. Normally, he would not have been present, since unlike his Adversary the Creator, he could not be everywhere at once. Instead, he depended upon those underneath him, to carry out their devilish duties while he roamed to and fro, seeking whom he may devour.

This was a special gathering, however, with an agenda that involved a particular thorn in the Evil Man's side. Calling for order, he spoke above the cacophony. "Quiet! Listen up, if you value what is left of your miserable lives." Turning to one of his closest advisors, a general in the demon army, he asked, "Is it true what I heard, that the one known as Friend is being called off the trail?"

"Yes, my Lord," the demon answered. "Our observers saw him with the one called Jake. They spoke, and the pilgrim was told to go to the mountain." With an evil smile he added, "And he was told to go alone."

Think about this:

If you believe you can go through life as 'Switzerland', avoiding association with the spiritual powers around you, think again. You are, at the end of the day, a spiritual creation who for a short time on this earth inhabits a physical body. The very fact that you are God's most precious creation places you right in the sights of the enemy who wants nothing better than to see you fail. The question for you today is not, 'Who am I?' but 'Whose am I?'

Now if you are unwilling to serve the LORD, choose this day whom you will serve, whether the gods your ancestors served in the region beyond the river or the gods of the Amorites in whose land you are living; but as for me and my household, we will serve the LORD."

Joshua 24:15

Episode Five
At the Trailhead

Friend had been walking in silence most of the day. He tried to pray, but all that escaped his lips were deep sighs that were not simply the product of the heavy pack he carried. He couldn't erase the image of his dear wife, standing back at the campsite, crying uncontrollably. Watching her grief was like razor blades rolling around in his gut. He wondered if a man could actually die from grief itself? As his breath came in short gasps and his heart seemed to be on the verge of bursting with each tortured beat, he thought, *Yes, I could die right here. In fact, that would be a wonderful mercy, to put an end to this exquisite pain, right here and now*. And that realization helped him understand that he would *not* be dying... not here. Not now. He had been told to climb to the top of the mountain, and a lifetime of pilgrimage had taught him that God always gives strength to do what He lays before a traveler. Perhaps there was some good in this grief, after all; something to be learned. Something to be shared. Something that would make him a better man.

But not now. With his eyes focused on the ground slowly passing underneath his feet, Friend had to come to the realization that he was in no condition right now to learn anything. He had nothing to share, and without a doubt he was not becoming a 'better man'. Not now. Maybe not ever. All he was feeling was the strength to put one foot in front of the other, just like he and his wife were reading from Isaiah 40:31 this morning.

They shall walk and not faint.

Gotta starting living what I preach, Friend thought to himself. *I haven't fainted yet, and I guess that's the promise.* Running and flying might come later — or maybe not — but for today, for right now, he was walking. And that was enough.

The thought caused him to raise his eyes away from his feet and look ahead. *Divine timing*, he thought with the first grin that had escaped his lips today. *If I'd kept my eyes glued to the ground, I might have missed the turnoff.* There, not ten paces ahead, was a fork in the trail. The more well-worn path to the left was obviously the main route. If there was any doubt, it was erased by the small sign on the right side marking the cut off.

'By Invitation Only', the sign read. Adjusting his pack straps, Friend took a deep breath and stepped up slightly onto the path that would lead to the top of the mountain, and almost at once noticed someone blocking his way. For a brief instant, he was surprised, then recognition swept over him and he felt the adrenalin rushing into every part of his body. He scanned the area surrounding the stranger who stood in the middle of the path just ahead. He seemed to be alone. With a discernment developed over the years, Friend spoke up.

"What? No cuddly sheep this time to convince me to turn back? I don't see your invitation, by the way. Does God know that you're here, or are you hoping He won't notice?"

Friend saw the faint twitch in the eyes of the stranger, but he recovered quickly. "Sheep are for children. And you, my Friend, are anything but a child."

"I'm no friend of yours, as you well know. Now, are you going to step aside and let me pass, or challenge me? Whatever you do, get on with it. I'd like to cover more ground before dark."

"That's what I've always liked about you," the stranger said with a smile. "You're a man on a mission. No one and nothing will deter you from doing what… you *think*… is right."

"Oh, so you're suggesting that this is not the right path I'm on? Have I somehow missed the command? And by the way," Friend continued, "I don't believe you're the one they call *Anger*, are you? What happened? Did he miss the cut this time?"

"Anger is a fool," the stranger spat. "His antics are only for those too weak to understand their own actions. He will not be coming this time."

"Oh! So there is a *this* time? Who are you, and what do you have to offer me?"

"My name is not important," the stranger began. "I have other—"

"No. You have nothing," Friend interrupted him. "But you do have a responsibility, given not by the Evil Man who pulls your strings, but by *me*, who speaks by the authority of the One Who sends me here. In the Name of Jesus Christ, God's Son and my Savior: what is your name?"

A small bead of sweat broke out across the brow of the stranger, and he looked quickly from one side to the other, as if searching for one who might either help or hurt him. Seeing neither, he spoke as he had been commanded. "I am known as Denial, but I do not come to you today as I did before. When you were young and desperate for any alternative to the loathsome task you had been given, I simply suggested that you and your son turn back and leave this mountain."

Getting a measure of composure back, he went on. "It was unfortunate that you failed to heed my plea. How might things have been different if you had not proceeded to the summit? The death of your only son… that *horrific* time in the swamp. I can't believe you actually ate rats to stay alive. And all because you felt it necessary to obey *Him*."

"I didn't *feel* in was necessary to obey, Demon. It *was* necessary. Truth is truth, regardless of how you feel about it. And at the end of the day, my son is with *Him*. And by His will, I'll be joining him in *His* Kingdom, which is more than I can say about you."

"So you say," Denial uttered with less conviction than he may have felt had he been standing before any other pilgrim on the path. "All I'm asking — and understand... I'm only *asking*. I know I could never command you to do anything — all I'm asking is that you look back over your years on this path. You are not that young and impetuous backpacker you once were. Time and miles have taught you well. You are now a strong and capable man. People look to you for leadership. Your family looks to you for love and support."

Denial took a step back as if to consider anew this pilgrim. "Look at you! You're strong! You're brave. You're in the prime of your life with so much more to offer! Is this the kind of man who still listens to someone who never shows himself to you, depending instead on underlings to act as messengers? Don't you think it's time to take the next logical step of a leader — to *lead*? Those who depend on you will rejoice to see their mentor stepping up with confidence, no longer moving blindly by the strings of an unseen puppeteer. This is what *He* fears, after all. Cut the strings and become like *Him.* You've earned your position. Turn back now and take your proper place."

"Funny you should mention those *underlings*," Friend observed. "I know Jake pretty well, and while he makes no apology for his unswerving loyalty to his Creator, I don't think he would take too kindly to being called an *underling* by someone like you." Friend looked over Denial's shoulder and went on, "Am I right, Jake?"

With those words, Denial jumped like he had been shot, turning to look behind him. There standing directly in the middle of the trail, leaning casually on a sword that rose to his breastplate, stood Jake. In answer, one eyebrow rose a fraction of an inch, and he smiled, first at Friend, then directly into the eyes of the demon called Denial. The effect was dramatic.

"I'm leaving!" Denial said, stumbling toward Friend, then sidestepping to get around him in his haste. "I'm only following orders. I would do nothing without the pilgrim's permission. He knows that! I'm just—"

"You're just an underling who does what he's told," Friend said. "So listen to what I'm telling you right now: in the Name of Jesus, be gone with you. And I don't want to see you again. Got it?"

Denial didn't answer, but in the blink of an eye, he was simply not there any more. Friend turned back to Jake and said with a renewed breath of air, "Thank you."

"Don't mention it," Jake replied. He turned to leave, then faced Friend again. "There will be more, you know. And I won't always be here."

"I know, Jake; I know. And you knew what I needed when I needed it. I'll try to do better now."

Jake grinned in response, gave a big wave with his sword and disappeared from view. Friend knew that he would not be accompanying him the rest of the way. The command was to go alone, after all. But he also knew that Jake and those like him would always be close by, providing what was needed, when it was needed.

That knowledge brought a new strength that he hadn't expected, and Friend continued on up the trail.

Think about this:

When difficulties come your way, and your strength is fading, do you ever feel alone? If so, remember all the times in God's Word where He reminds us that He is always near. Then rejoice!

The promise of His Presence is sometimes forgotten when events transpire that make it seem that we have been deserted. In the midst of battle, many a pilgrim has cried out, "Where are You Lord? I thought You would be here and fight with me. Have you led me to the battle line only to draw back and watch me die?"

If you have ever felt that way, remember that we live in a world broken by sin. As a child of God, our sin has been forgiven, but the scars of the Curse still remain. At times, God will step in and rescue His children, but on other occasions, He stays His Hand, and as a result, pilgrims are hurt and often die. Those left to watch are tempted to ask, "Where is God now? Why do His faithful children suffer?" If you or someone you know have experienced something like this, seek out those whose faith you can trust. Share with them. Pray with them. Hope with them. And when the time is right, rejoice with them.

He has said, "I will never leave you or forsake you." So we can say with confidence,

"The Lord is my helper; I will not be afraid. What can anyone do to me?"

Hebrews 13:5–6

Episode Six
Powers and Principalities Council

The mood was somber among those in attendance. The demon known as Denial had returned from his mission and was uncharacteristically quiet. Only Anger was smiling. He knew that Denial had failed in his task of turning the pilgrim back, and was gloating with undisguised delight. Denial had not reported to the Evil Man, because he knew that his attempt had been observed and reported back already. One look on the Chief Demon's face told him everything.

The Evil Man rose from his makeshift throne and looked out over the gathering. Denial's fellow deceivers were wisely quiet, knowing only that but for the grace of... well... of their lord and master, any one of them might be the focus of this present scrutiny. The Evil Man walked around the room, seemingly a random movement, but everyone could see that each step brought him closer to Denial, who was trying unsuccessfully to disappear among the crowd. When the Chief Demon was close enough that his hot breath could be felt, Denial spoke up.

"It wasn't my fault!" he said almost in a whimper. "The pilgrim summoned an angelic army! I had no chance!"

"You know of course that you were being observed. If I were you, I would choose my words carefully. *Angelic army*, you say? The way I heard it, there was only one, standing alone on the trail. Not threatening you. Not making any move toward you. He was… what did I hear? Smiling at you. Oh! And he raised an eyebrow. Yes, very frightening indeed. Terrifying."

"But that wasn't all," Denial went on, cringing all the more. The pilgrim called… he called… He called on the name… the name of—"

"*Stop!*" the Evil Man shouted. "You utter those words at your peril. The bottom line is, you failed. I gave you a task to accomplish, and you failed in that task, choosing instead to run away. And here you are. Tell me, *Denial*, do you feel safe here? Am I less to be feared than an old man with a sword, *smiling* at you?"

"But you weren't there, my Lord! You didn't see his face. You didn't hear the pilgrim, and the words he spoke. No one could have stood before that. No one."

"And that is precisely why I sent you, a deceiver with many a soul under his belt. I would have thought that someone like you would have been able to persuade that mortal to turn back from his mission without forcing his hand. That's what deceivers do, after all, isn't it? You confront an unsuspecting traveler, take them into your confidence, and lead them, ever so gently away from their appointed task. No need for bloodshed, nor for unnecessary discomfort. Your forte is... *was*... denial. Simply convince your victims to contradict what they thought was true. Lead them away from the path, one soft step at a time. But I can see now that you are incapable of such subtlety. Perhaps you would have more success among them," he said, pointing with his chin toward the pack of demon warriors. They were obviously having trouble following the conversation, but could see that it was not going well for the poor deceiver. This brought a chorus of shouts and grunts followed by a cacophony of war clubs being slammed into the ground.

"No, my Lord! Have mercy! Please let me retain my place among the council. I am still a force to be contended with. Look at my record, and know that many, *many* have fallen under my deceits. And there will be many more. I promise you."

The Evil Man was silent for what seemed like an eternity. Then the hint of a smile broke over one side of his mouth. "Perhaps," he said looking over to the chamchas who were taking this all in with relish, thankful only that it was not them under the spotlight. "Perhaps you may still have a measure of usefulness to me. Leave me now, and find another pilgrim who is not quite so *formidable* to you. Show me what you can do, then I will make my decision."

With a string of blubbering words that sounded reminiscent of a leaking water pipe, Denial backed away from the Evil Man, not stopping until he was outside the room, whereupon he turned and ran as fast as his spindly legs could carry him. Everyone watched him go, then turned back to face their lord and master. Finally, the deceiver known as Scapegoat spoke up.

"I have an idea that just might work," he said hesitantly.

"You've faced this man before, as I recall. And like Denial you too failed miserably."

"But he's a different man now," Scapegoat insisted. "And it's a different path that he walks. Before, he feared only for the life of his son. Now after so many years, he sees the world differently. I think I can use that to suggest something totally new to him; something he is not expecting."

"Going to keep us in suspense, eh?" the Evil Man commented. "Very well. Go. And don't return without the soul of the one they call *Friend*."

Think about this:

Keep in mind that, while this is a story of fiction, it is based upon certain truths that Scripture will affirm. First, remember that, just as the demon Denial was sent packing, neither do we stand helpless before the enemy's intentions for us. Satan's power may seem formidable, but don't forget that he has been defeated already. The Perfect Sacrifice of Jesus on the Cross sealed his fate. We *can* resist. We *can* come against him in the Name of Jesus.

But remember also that Satan is still around, like a bad dog on a short leash. He does not sleep, nor does he give up his task of trying to hurt God's most precious creation: you. Be watchful and be prepared always.

Put on the whole armor of God, so that you may be able to stand against the wiles of the devil. For our struggle is not against enemies of blood and flesh, but against the rulers, against the authorities, against the cosmic powers of this present darkness, against the spiritual forces of evil in the heavenly places. Ephesians 6:11–12

Episode Seven
On the Mountain Trail

Friend continued upward as the trail wound through a pine forest, then broke into a grove of aspen. Their leaves were beginning to turn yellow and gold, a sign of summer's end, soon to be followed by the coming winter. The bright colors sitting atop the white tree trunks were a welcome contrast to the dark evergreens he had left behind, and the sounds from the aspen leaves were almost like a song being lifted to the sun as it made its way down to the horizon. On any other day, the sights and sounds would have brought joy to the pilgrim's heart, but as evening approached, he kept thinking back to his encounter with the demon called Denial. The experience was a clear win, Friend was sure, but it left him wounded at heart.

The temptation had been simple enough: turn around and go back. Why set out on such a horrible journey, except for the fact that *He* had commanded it? And, of course, that was answer enough. Over the years, Friend had made countless decisions based on nothing more than that he was convinced it was God's will. True, he had never actually faced his Creator, as Denial had reminded him. But instead, he had depended upon fellow pilgrims whose faith he trusted, or upon the word of Jake, an angelic messenger whom he had no reason to doubt. And besides, there was that constant stirring in his heart that he now understood to be the Presence of God Himself in the form of the promised Comforter. It was a concept that he never fully understood but was required to accept by faith. And that faith had never failed him.

But oh, how weak he was! Despite a lifetime of affirmation and joy; despite day after day of unmistakable evidence of his Creator's Presence and the countless promises that gave him hope and assurance, all it took was one demonic deceiver who did nothing but plant a seed of doubt. "You could be back in the arms of your loving wife this very night," he was told. "Those who depend on your strength, those who call you 'Mentor' would be so happy to see you return. And it's so easy: just turn around and go back. Be a real leader, for once. Make a decision for yourself."

Of course Friend did not fall victim to such bold-faced lies. He knew this journey was Divinely ordained, and no amount of rationalizing would diminish his determination to stay the course. But still…

Then there was Jake. His appearance had been perfectly timed, and the result was dramatic. What Friend would have given for another glimpse at the face of Denial when he saw the warrior standing there, relaxed but vigilant! *Yep, I'm on the winning side, for sure*, Friend thought to himself. But then Jake had reminded him that he wouldn't always be there to intervene. This was a journey he had been told to make alone. And both Jake and the demon had said that there would be more encounters like this, farther up the trail. And worse ones, he was convinced. If something like *this* left him so scarred, what would the next one bring? Would he be able to stand up to whatever the Evil Man might throw at him, alone?

Looking around, Friend noticed that he was nearing the edge of the aspen grove. What waited beyond was more pine, mixed with cedar and fir, more tightly packed together as he gained altitude. It seemed as if even the trees could sense the increasing altitude that brought with it more threats to their survival. And so they huddled together, united against the elements that wanted to deny their existence here. More than ever, Friend wished for another living thing to cling to. Looking up, he saw the first stars of the evening making their appearance. It was getting dark, and the path ahead would be darker still. Time to stop for the night. Maybe a little rest and the rising sun would restore him.

His wife had packed him some meals that didn't require heating, but something in the air told Friend that he would need a fire that night. He was still on the lower slopes of the mountain, not yet high enough to have reached the thermal belt between the cold air in the valley and the colder temperatures on the heights. It was going to be freezing tonight. And dark. Gathering some of the soft aspen wood, he made a campfire, banking it up on one side so that the heat would reflect toward his sleeping bag. Experience over the years had taught him to build his fires small. This would not only conserve firewood, but would also allow him to sit nearer the flames, soaking up the precious warmth. But as the wood began to catch and define the circle of light around him, Friend found himself piling on more and more wood. The crackling of the flames served as a kind of companion, drowning out the sounds of the forest around him and drawing him closer as to a faithful traveling companion.

Pulling out a sandwich from his backpack, he felt a lump building in his throat, remembering the loving hands that had prepared it for him. He recalled his last view of her that morning, standing dutifully at their campsite, crying uncontrollably at the thought that she would never see her precious husband again, at least not in this life. Suddenly the emotions could not be held in check any more, and Friend let the sandwich fall to the ground as the tears came. No need to be brave any more. You're a child of God, he reminded himself. Be a kid and cry your heart out.

He cried until there were no more tears left to shed, then simply sat and allowed the sobbing to continue, his body wracked with a pain so exquisite that he felt he could never be consoled. He remembered times, so many years ago, when his son or his daughter had cried like this. The reasons for the tears had long ago been forgotten, but the experience would be forever burned into his memory. They had cried like children who had lost everything and would not be comforted in spite of his soothing words and loving arms. *I wonder if God feels like that right now?* he wondered. *I know He loves me. Surely, my pain does not escape His heart.* He remembered the words of Matthew 10:29. *Are not two sparrows sold for a penny? Yet not one of them will fall to the ground apart from your Father.*

"That's me," Friend confessed to himself. "I'm falling to the ground, wounded and bleeding." Sitting there in front of the fire, clutching his knees and feeling the dampness on his jeans from a waterfall of tears, he sat still and waited, wishing for death to come. But instead, he remembered the rest of that passage. *So do not be afraid; you are of more value than many sparrows.*

Gradually, Friend's sobbing turned to prayers. At first, they were nothing more than nonsense syllables from a heart too torn to think of anything more. But they were enough to be carried all the way to the throne of God by the Comforter. There, according to the promise in Romans 8:26, *Likewise the Spirit helps us in our weakness; for we do not know how to pray as we ought, but that very Spirit intercedes with sighs too deep for words.*

And as the intercession continued, the answers to Friend's prayer found their way back into his heart. And instead of meaningless utterances, they came as words, a continuation of the passage from Romans. *Don't you know, my Child? Neither death, nor life, nor angels, nor rulers, nor things present, nor things to come, nor powers, nor height, nor depth, nor anything else in all creation, will be able to separate you from My love.*

As the words made their way into Friend's consciousness, he took a deep breath, the first in several minutes. Letting the air out of his lungs, words began forming. Words of praise, of thankfulness. Words of hope and joy. In the next moment, he was lying on his side, facing the fire that in spite of the soft and quick-burning wood had not diminished its flame. Throughout the rest of the night, it burned brightly, spreading its warmth into every fiber of Friend's being. His sleep was sweet and restoring.

On the outskirts of the camp, just beyond the circle of light, an army of demons stood, poised to sweep over the weeping pilgrim in the midst of his grief. But as much as they gripped their swords and snarled in defiance, they could not move forward. Held back by a Force as invisible as they themselves were to the world, and yet more powerful than anything ever devised by Man or Spirit, they could only cry out in frustration at their inability to vent their rage. And they continued to rage all through the night, unheard by the sleeping pilgrim, who rested in Perfect Peace.

Think about this:

When was the last time you cried — *really* cried — as a child who would not be comforted? Those tears did not go unnoticed by your Heavenly Father. Your pain and suffering are reflected in His own Heart; He takes no pleasure in the grief of His children. But sometimes such pain is a necessary thing, bringing us a deeper understanding of who we really are and *whose* we will always be. When your heart demands tears, let them come. Use that time to feel the Presence of God. Let His words of comfort find their way to the deepest part of your soul. And may those words bring you peace, and healing, and a new direction for your journey, carrying you all the way to those Divine heights that wait to welcome you.

And if I go and prepare a place for you, I will come again and will take you to myself, so that where I am, there you may be also. And you know the way to the place where I am going.
John 14:3–4

Episode Eight
Morning Breaks

The sun came up early this high on the mountain's slope, and with it brought a gentle breeze, pushing the cold night air up and through the aspen leaves. The resulting chorus was like a heavenly choir to Friend's ears. His sleep had been exceptionally good, and he was surprised to find enough heat left in the campfire to warm a cup of coffee. "Thank you, Lord," he said as he sipped from the steaming mug, then remembered that he had said the same thing just twenty-four hours ago, before Jake's fateful visit. So much had happened since then.

His midsection still hurt from last night's uncontrolled sobbing, but as he rubbed his aching muscles, Friend thought, *This is what they mean when they call something a good kinda hurt*. The grief was still there, down deep, and he knew it would take no more than a moment of reflection to bring it back to the surface. But for the moment, a new day was dawning, God was still on His throne, and he could still enjoy hot coffee!

Packing up his sleeping bag, he kicked at the ashes to make sure the fire was completely out. As he did, he looked over at the firewood supply he had stacked nearby and was mildly surprised to see it hadn't been used at all, in spite of the fact that he had been warmed all night by the flames, and rewarded this morning with just enough for hot water. *Aspen wood is soft*, he thought, wondering again how it could burn so long. But the musing was soon replaced with thoughts of the trail and what might be waiting around the next bend.

The next few miles passed in a gradual climb, moving through the pines and cedars, then another grove of aspen trees. The sound of water reached his ears, and though it was still far away, he could tell it was a distant waterfall. In spite of the altitude-induced chill in the air, Friend was sweating from the exertion of the climb. A cold shower might be a welcome break, he thought. The trail led steadily upwards, then took two switchbacks that led over a knife-edged ridge. Reaching the high point of the ridge, he was able to look into a deep canyon on the other side. At the apex of the canyon, a waterfall was making its way over a jumble of rocks that had apparently blocked a small stream farther up the slope. The water had collected as long as it could, then broke out over the top in a spectacular display, falling at least a hundred feet to a clear pool below. From his vantage point, he could see that the trail would take him down to the pool, then up the other side of the ridge and on toward the top.

After half an hour of negotiating the switchbacks leading down the steep slope, Friend finally arrived at the pool. Testing the water, he confirmed that it was indeed as cold as ice. Nevertheless, he took his shirt off and leaned over into the cascade, rewarded with a stab of pain followed by a wonderful refreshing that made the exertion of getting there worth the effort. Finding a small spot of sunlight, he stretched out on the grass and let the warm rays dry him off. The sensation was delicious, and he was almost lulled into a mid-morning nap. It was interrupted though when a shadow came between him and the sun. Friend opened his eyes and immediately came awake and to his feet. There stood a man dressed in the normal gear of a hiker, but instead of the insulated down jacket that would have been expected along the trail, he was wearing a sheepskin coat. The effect was to give him the image of a lamb standing on his two hind legs, and it was that picture that gave Friend the insight to discern who the man was.

"If I'm not mistaken, we've met before, on this same mountain. You offered to take the place of my son. Become the required sacrifice and serve as my *Scapegoat*."

"You have an excellent eye, Friend," Scapegoat answered. He took a step closer, which caused Friend to step back involuntarily, reaching for the sword he no longer carried. "No need for unpleasantries, pilgrim. I bear no grudge for the way you treated me last time. We were both much younger then, eh?"

"I suppose you're referring to my grabbing you and trying to take a knife to your throat. We both knew you had no intention of fulfilling your promise of dying in the place of my son. All you wanted then was what you undoubtedly want now — to see me turn back and leave this mountain."

"As I said, we were both much younger," said Scapegoat. "Believe me when I say that I only wanted you to avoid the horrible events that did in fact transpire. In your ignorance, you could only understand that your son was suffering, and that someone needed to be a substitute. I merely offered to be that replacement. Whether or not I actually followed through was between myself and *Him*," he said, with a quick glimpse toward the summit. "All you had to do was turn back, your son would have lived and you would have enjoyed many more years of parental bliss with him."

"If you believe that," Friend cautioned, "then we need to ask ourselves who in fact is the more immature between us. Leaving the path God places before us never ends well... as I'm sure you know." Reaching for his backpack, Friend made as if to leave. "But enough of this mindless chatter. I have miles to go before the day is finished. So as I reminded your pal *Denial*, I must now say..."

"Wait!" Scapegoat interrupted with a shout. "Stop, please. Just let me say what I came to say, then I will leave you to your unfortunate fate."

I'm going to regret this, Friend thought to himself. "Very well, speak your mind. I'm not afraid of your lies. Not any more."

With a silent breath of relief, *Scapegoat* spoke quickly. "I do not deny that I serve the enemy of your master. Anything I may have suggested back then or even today are only the result of my devotion to him."

"Well, well, a little honesty for a change," Friend observed. "But don't think that I will let my guard down because of it."

"Quite the contrary," Scapegoat interjected. "I would like to see you redouble your guard... and to have a clear view of those who actually threaten you. My concern is that you have been led to an understanding of *justice* that may be ill-conceived.

"Think back to that time so many years ago but not far from here, where we are now standing. You had been told to take your son to the mountaintop and there watch him die as a sacrifice to *Him.*"

Even now, Scapegoat could not bring himself to utter the Name.

"All I did was to offer myself as a substitute for your son: to be the scapegoat in his place. And you had no problem with the concept. You were perfectly willing to allow me to take his place; or if I was unwilling to drag my carcass to the altar.

"But listen: *who* in fact was the scapegoat? Who had done no wrong and yet was being led to a cruel and unjust death? Your son! And now, years have passed. You have suffered greatly, trying to appease *Him*. And for what? To climb this wretched mountain once again, to leave behind your friends and family and allow yourself to be yet another sacrifice. I tell you, Pilgrim, *you* are the scapegoat. You are the required victim.

"And your friends and your family will grieve. They will mourn and cry and lament your passing... and as the tears fade, they will say to themselves, *It was a good death.*"

"What are you talking about, Demon?" Friend bristled. "I am not climbing this mountain in order to be a 'sacrifice' for anyone. And neither was my son. We live in a broken world, a world your master helped break. It's appointed us once to die, and after that, the judgment. And that's an appointment none of us will miss, including you."

"We'll see about that," Scapegoat said with a smile. "But remember that in the meantime, the world is still 'broken', as you say — not by the hand of my master, by the way, but by Adam and those who came after him — and each and every wrong must be punished. Even a child knows that. And if you can avoid the slayer's hand by the sending of a substitute, a *scapegoat*, then inwardly you will be relieved. Only this time, the lot has fallen on you, pilgrim. *You* are the scapegoat today."

"So that's it then?" Friend asked. "Death is inevitable, and this time you're not offering to take my place?"

"Death is not inevitable," Scapegoat shot back. "In your ignorance and weakness, you blindly follow whatever *He* tells you. You cry and grieve when your friends and family are led away to the altar, and when your turn comes, you insist that it's only the doorway to another, wonderful life. Who do you know that has passed through that veil and returned to assure you that what you have believed all your life is true? And don't try and tell me about *Him* and his *Son*. They are in it together, can't you see?"

Scapegoat waited for a reply, and when none came, he spoke in a softer tone. "All I'm trying to do is save you from all this totally unnecessary pain and suffering. And I am not alone. There are many of us who have seen *Him* for who he really is. We are many, I assure you. And we are led by seasoned powers, hardened on the battlefield and ready to stand and fight."

Turning slightly to face the waterfall, Scapegoat continued, "Like him."

Think about this:

The human side of us recognizes that every wrong must be made right. This is what 'justice' is all about and fools and lawbreakers would try to avoid it. But the good news is this: justice has been met by the Son of God. By His blood, spilt on the Cross, you and I can approach His throne forgiven and cleansed. But so often we forget that reality and continue to live under the shadow of guilt. The enemy knows this, and is ready and willing to offer us a way to be free from our sin, even though that way has already been bought and paid for. The next time you are weighed down by the burden you carry, look to the One who loves you: the one who says gently, "Lay it down, My child."

"Come to me, all you that are weary and are carrying heavy burdens, and I will give you rest. Take my yoke upon you, and learn from me; for I am gentle and humble in heart, and you will find rest for your souls. For my yoke is easy, and my burden is light."

Matthew 11:28–30

Episode Nine
The Demon General

"All I'm trying to do is save you from all this totally unnecessary pain and suffering," Scapegoat insisted. "And I am not alone. There are many of us who have seen *Him* for who he really is. We are many, I assure you. And we are led by seasoned powers, hardened on the battlefield and ready to stand and fight."

Turning slightly to face the waterfall, Scapegoat continued, "Like him."

From a dark crevice behind the waterfall that Friend had not noticed before, a man emerged. No, he thought again; it was not a man. It was yet another demon who could only have come from the depths of Hell itself. His skin was almost reptilian in appearance, reminding Friend of the club-swinging brutes he had encountered along the trail; but this creature's eyes told a different story. This was no dumb beast who knew only the basest of emotions — usually involving hatred and revenge — the thing that stood before Friend had a look that was positively terrifying. A scar slashed across his face, just missing his nose by a fraction and removing much of the protective flesh around his right eye. But the eye still functioned, and at that moment, both eyes were staring intently at Friend with a look that bordered between perfect hatred and imperfect hope: hope that all was not in fact lost.

"Scapegoat is an idiot," the demon began, "but on this point he is correct. You are *not* alone. You are part of a vast army. From every tribe, every nation, every generation, a host is being drawn together for the greatest confrontation of all time. The only thing left for you to decide, *pilgrim*, is upon which side you stand."

In spite of the terror that threatened to drive Friend to his knees, he began to speak with a confidence he did not in fact feel. "That issue was settled long ago. I serve the One True God. And He will have the victory."

The demon's eyes crinkled into what might have been either a smile or the prelude to rage. "You seem bold for one who has never met his commander face to face. Brave for one who has not had the opportunity to look over the battlefield as I have and seen the overwhelming superiority *I* command. I see the response in your eyes, *pilgrim*. You think just because "*He* decrees victory, that makes it so? Look around you. Can you find any corner of the universe where your kind has the upper hand? From the smallest hamlet to the grandest nation, *my* followers rule. Even in those places you call 'fortresses of faith', I have my own fifth column in place; men and women who profess to be believers but in the depths of their hearts cling to what I have promised them: freedom from *His* tyranny."

The demon took a step closer and lowered his voice as if for Friend's ears alone. "And even if the tide turned against us, I can turn to *Him* and say, 'Condemn us if you will, but remember that these poor souls are your very own, bought with the blood of your son. If you intend to cast us into the lake of fire, remember that you are casting out your most precious creation as well.'

"Do you think your god will do that? I think not."

The more the demon spoke, the more Friend felt his strength sapping away. This thing was his kryptonite. It was time to end this. "I will hear no more! By the One Whose Name I bear, I—"

Suddenly the demon was right in Friend's face, so that he could feel the hot breath and smell the sulfurous stench that came from his nostrils. "Hear me well, for I will not repeat it: if you open your mouth to speak another word, I will remove your head from your shoulders so quickly you will not see it coming. Keep in mind that here you stand alone before me. Even your friend Jake warned you that he would not be coming to your rescue. What you choose to do — or not do — right now, right here, is entirely in your hands. Join us, or suffer a fate you cannot begin to comprehend."

In response, Friend took a step backward. He knew better than to look around for help. There would be none. He had been placed in the crucible and found wanting. He took another step backward and was barely aware of the icy water filling his shoes. He tried to speak, but no words would come. A third step backward sent him reeling into the river, soaking him to the bone and providing just enough shock to enable his continued retreat.

"Your action speaks your decision, *pilgrim*. Remember that from this moment on, you are mine. Under my authority and subject to my command. Now, leave this mountain and wait for my orders."

Think about this:

Even the bravest of God's children can be terror-struck in the face of the enemy. By the very fact that they are not of this world, our senses are easily victimized by the 'shock and awe' that comes with any demonic revelation. Do you remember the first words that are always spoken whenever an angel of the Lord has appeared to men? *Fear not*. Satan's minions offer no such comfort. By their demeanor and by their words, they say to us, *Be afraid. Be very afraid*. There are times when we can and should resist such deceptions, answering in the Name of Jesus and moving forward in the confidence that you stand under His banner.

There are also times when God's Word tells us to run. It is not the act of a coward but of an obedient warrior who moves where his Master leads. Today as you face whatever comes your way, remember to pick your battles, led by God's Holy Spirit, Who lives and works with you.

Run for dear life from evil; hold on for dear life to good.

Romans 12:9 (*The Message*)

Episode Ten
Powers and Principalities Council

The Evil Man was in the process of sending chamchas, deceivers and demon warriors out on different missions, all designed to wreak havoc upon pilgrims moving along the trail, when Scapegoat entered the hall. The Evil Man noticed and raised his voice, to beckon him near. "Scapegoat! Come and give an accounting."

As he drew closer to the front of the room under the careful scrutiny of everyone present, the Evil Man continued, "So my observers report that you had a conversation with the pilgrim; also, that you prevented him from saying the words that would have forced you to leave, even if it meant that you had to... beg... just a little."

"It was not 'begging', I assure you, my Lord. It was merely a strategic move to gain his confidence." Scapegoat hoped that the Evil Man could not see his legs as they trembled at the recollection of that terrible moment.

"And in another surprising move, you convinced one of my generals to join you there at the waterfall. And the two of you managed to heap upon the one called

Friend what seemed to be a brilliant concoction of deceit and raw fear.

"And yet... here you are, *without* the pilgrim's soul, as I commanded. What do you have to say, Scapegoat?"

"Only that my plan is proceeding beyond even my own expectations. What the observers did not report back to you, my Lord, is that this encounter was only the first in a series of moves that the pilgrim will be quite incapable of resisting. Even as we speak, he is wandering off the trail in abject terror, each step taking him farther and farther from the mountain's summit."

The Evil Man's eyebrows rose a fraction. "I had not heard of that outcome. Be assured that I will be checking the facts more closely, and when I am done, *someone* will suffer. I trust it will not be you, for giving me inaccurate information."

"What I have just spoken is quite true, my Lord, and can easily be confirmed. The one called Friend has by his silence agreed to join our side. Now he is stumbling through the forest grieving over past decisions and trying to come to grips with the new realities I have shown him. "But my plans for him have only begun," Scapegoat said with an evil grin. "Before I am done with him, he will be cursing our enemy and swearing allegiance to you... All for naught, of course. The fool thinks we would even want him in our ranks."

Scapegoat took a step closer, evidence of his renewed confidence. "No, in one moment — a moment that will be witnessed by all in this great council — the pilgrim will be driven to his knees in despair, understanding finally the gravity of his error and the consequences of his disobedience. Once we are finished with his total humiliation, then we will allow him to go on to his fate. Although," Scapegoat concluded with a laugh, "I think by now he will not be so kindly received by the one to whom he has paid such homage all these years.

"And here is the best part, my Lord. Such dishonor and degradation will be affirmed by all in this room, and *You*, Oh Great One, will be credited for his eternal undoing. We will let the pilgrim wander awhile longer, growing weaker with each step, then we will offer — and immediately withdraw — yet another ray of hope. Finally, he will find himself kneeling before you, in the presence of all these witnesses, where you will then decree to him whatever my Lord decides. You will have your vengeance, and before these, you will have your glory."

The Evil Man stood silently for several moments, contemplating what he had just heard. Finally, he spoke. "Scapegoat, if what you tell me is true, then you have truly outdone yourself. Until this project is finished, this will be your only priority. Don't let the pilgrim out of your sight. If anyone tries to interfere or mount some kind of rescue, see to it that they fail. My warriors and their generals are at your disposal. But hear me well, Scapegoat: if you dare and try any of your deceptions on *me*, or if for any reason you fail in this task, imagine if you will the worst possible punishment you have ever seen me mete out, and know for a fact it would be far, far preferable to what I will heap on you. Now go, and report back to me the time and place this council will gather to witness my greatest victory over that loathsome one they call *Friend*."

Think about this:

Going all the way back to the Garden of Eden, the sin of Pride has been mankind's greatest undoing. *...and you will be like God, knowing good and evil* (Genesis 3:5b). Feelings of pride can drive us to life's greatest accomplishments, even as those same feelings drive us to our destruction.

But remember this, Satan is also driven by pride, and just as we are condemned by it, so also he is being led to his own eternal judgment because of it. Pride in itself it not evil; even the Apostle Paul insisted that he had *reason to boast of my work for God* (Romans 15:17). We have been wonderfully made, with the potential for great deeds in the Name of our Lord. But just as Paul knew the Source of his abilities, may we also remember, and *stand in awe* (Romans 11:20), giving praise to Whom it is due.

I will boast all the more gladly of my weaknesses, so that the power of Christ may dwell in me.
2 Corinthians 12:19

Episode 11
Despair

The sun was growing dimmer along the shady side of the mountain, making it increasingly difficult to see where his feet were falling. But Friend took no notice. He neither knew nor cared where he was going, his mind overwhelmed with a mixture of terror and regret. He had experienced numerous encounters with demonic powers over the years and along the path, but the Satanic general was like nothing he could have imagined, even in his worst nightmares. Here was a being who seemed to hold absolute power over all the hordes of princes and principalities, except perhaps the Evil Man himself. And along with the display of power was an unquestioning confidence in his supremacy over every other spirit, including God.

Most frightening of all was Friend's inability to come against the demon with the Name of Jesus, hearing instead the threat of having his head removed before he could speak the words that would drive away any power that did not come from his Creator. Could he really do that? Friend wondered. *Well, I guess I'll never know*, he thought in his misery, *since I kept silent, backing myself into the river instead.*

The general's parting words still haunted Friend as he stumbled through the growing darkness. "Your action speaks your decision, *pilgrim*. Remember that from this moment on, you are mine. Under my authority and subject to my command. Now, leave this mountain and wait for my orders."

Could it be true? Have I committed the unthinkable? By my silence in the face of the enemy have I rejected my place in God's Kingdom and put myself under the authority of that... thing?

In different circumstances, Friend might have been able to think more clearly. Instead, he continued his decline, stumbling over rocks and tree stumps, adding to the wounds he already carried all over his body. The soaking from the river brought with it a chill that found its way into the farthest reaches, even into his heart. Finally, he fell headlong, remaining on his face in abject misery, too far gone even to cry.

And lurking all around him were a cohort of chamchas, waiting for just this moment. On any other day, they would have been routed by a single Word. But now they were free to do their worst, inflicting on the helpless pilgrim all they intended.

The sound of distant thunder could be heard just beyond the mountain, but not by Friend. Neither could he feel the drops of rain that began to fall all around him. He did feel a new sensation of pain, however, beginning at the base of his skull and encompassing his head in a vice-like grip that soon overshadowed every other ache.

Soon to follow was the heat: a feverish burning that invaded every joint in his body, competing with the massive headache for the attention that Friend was both unwilling and unable to bring to bear. He lay there instead, soaking up the misery like a dry well, neither relishing it nor actively enduring it. He simply lay there, one step away from death.

Think about this:

Look carefully at Friend's digression into absolute despair. First, he allowed the deceiver known as Scapegoat to have a conversation. Friend even said it himself: "I'm going to regret this." His misgivings were overlooked by his confidence, even going so far as to say to the demon, "I'm not afraid of your lies any more."

Scapegoat's deception led to doubt on the part of the pilgrim, suggesting that pain and suffering were not inevitable but instead were the result of a cruel God, helped by a malicious Son. Given time, perhaps Friend could have seen through the lie, but the demon general would not allow it, adding to the ruse and underscoring it with pure terror. What followed was an unrelenting fall into darkness, accompanied by growing doubt and physical deterioration, opening the way for further demonic attack. As you consider the story today, pray for wisdom to avoid even first contact with the enemy's plans for you, pray that you will not drop your guard, even when you feel confident, and pray for courage in the face of unfounded fear. Never underestimate the Scapegoat. He will serve as no one's sacrifice. He is a predator.

Be strong and of good courage. Do not be afraid or dismayed before the king of Assyria and all the horde that is with him; for there is one greater with us than with him.

2 Chronicles 32:7

Episode 12
Powers and Principalities Council

Scapegoat, who had been waiting anxiously by the door, noticed at once when an observer entered. He made his way quickly to the newcomer, they whispered for a moment, then Scapegoat approached the Evil Man.

"Good news, my Lord," he said. "The pilgrim is completely broken. Now is the time for you to exact your revenge upon him, while all your followers watch in awe."

The Evil Man gave Scapegoat a rare smile, then turned to face the gathering. "The pilgrim known as Friend has learned the folly of rejecting my authority. I'm going now to remind him of his foolishness and watch as he slips into oblivion. This is truly a time for rejoicing, and I invite all of you to accompany me to the mountain!"

With shouts of praise and acclamation, the company of demons began moving out of the room, the deceivers leading the way as one of their own basked in his victory. Following them were the demonic warriors, never completely understanding the situation but knowing only that the master was happy and so should they be. The chamchas, those who had not gone out already to torment the pilgrim, mixed in with the crowd and joined in the celebration. The Evil Man, watching the procession, turned to one of his close advisors and said in a low voice, "See to it that we are not opposed by *Him* and those who carry the name of his son. Remind the angel Jake, if you see him, that the pilgrim has renounced his faith and will be standing with us from this point on."

"Do you really intend to grant the pilgrim a place among our ranks?" the advisor asked with some surprise.

"Of course not, you idiot. But I want everyone on both sides to believe he is one of ours. Then when we've taken every advantage of that falsehood, I will cast the pilgrim away from my presence, leaving him with no master, no purpose and no reason for hope." The Evil Man let a small chuckle escape his lips, then said, "What pure joy, to see one of *His* precious ones slip into their own private hell."

Think about this:

Some might still insist that Friend does not deserve such torment from the enemy of this world, since all he has ever wanted was to walk the path set before him by God. He did not seek confrontation with demonic powers nor did he actively work to oppose them, but rather only responded when he himself came under attack by the Evil Man and those who do his bidding.

But let us not forget that, by virtue of the fact that we are so loved by God, we are and will remain the object of Satan's wrath. Words that we read with such comfort and assurance, such as John 3:16, serve only to remind him that his rebellion against the Heavenly Kingdom served to place him under an eternal curse that will find its ultimate fulfillment in a lake of fire.

Make no mistake: there is no neutral ground between God and Satan. By your declaration, or by your silence, you identify with one or the other. If you have never considered that fact, don't let the sun go down today before you affirm along with Joshua (24:15), *as for me and my house, we will serve the Lord.*

Some take pride in chariots, and some in horses, but our pride is in the name of the LORD our God.

Psalms 20:7

Episode 13
Under the Curse

Friend lay without moving, still face down in the dirt that was quickly becoming mud under an increasing rain. He neither heard nor acknowledged the distant thunder that promised even more. Neither did he hear the approaching hordes of demons as they vied for position around him, straining to see this broken and despairing pilgrim. The Evil Man stepped out from among them and came closer. For a long time, he just stood there staring, a cruel smile on his lips. Finally, he spoke.

"Never have I seen a man so crushed by his poor choices. And make no mistake: you have brought this on yourself."

Friend twitched at the sound of the Evil Man's voice, but made no move to respond.

"I think the worst part of all this is the deception, wouldn't you say?" the Evil Man said in a voice that sounded almost sympathetic. "To fall for the proposition that *He* actually loves you, in spite of all the evidence to the contrary. And then there's all that blather about a *Son*, and a divine plan to rescue you… if only you give *Him* everything."

The Evil Man stepped closer as if to share a secret. "It was a bold move on your part, I must admit. In spite of family, friends, and a whole world of contrary opinion, you risked it all for the sake of the prize. And you lost. And here you lie, face down in your own filth, without a friend, without family, without anyone who cares whether you live or die.

"Except for me." He was quiet for several moments; even the demons dared not breathe. Friend opened his eyes and looked around until he focused on the face of Evil. Suddenly the face broke into a hideous grin that turned to laughter. "And guess what? Even *I* don't care! You may have thought you had hope by coming to my camp, but listen, *Pilgrim*: there is no one in all of creation who loves you, or even likes you. You will die on this mountain with no one to mourn your passing.

"Now, you may be thinking, only a *very evil* person would refuse to take pity on the suffering. And you would be right... right in that I am a *very... evil... person*. Not only have I no sympathy for you; right at this moment, I have an almost desperate need to add to your suffering. I've started already, you know, by ordering my chamchas to invade every weakness you possess — and believe me, you have many — and to bring upon you every misery they can. Does your head hurt? How about your joints? Your very flesh? That's good, but I think I can improve even on that."

Friend heard a shuffling sound off to his left, and was able to turn his head just enough to see that a demon warrior was standing over him, grinning from ear to ragged and torn ear. The Evil Man spoke again. "I'm going to step back now, so that all my followers can see this. It will be a great lesson for anyone who might dare entertain the thought of opposing me." Turning to the warrior, he added, "Remember: only the knees. I want him awake and screaming."

The warrior took another step closer and moved his feet apart, to gain a better stance. Taking the huge club off his shoulder, he lowered it down in front of Friend's face, then moved it toward his feet. Giving one knee a tap with it that sent a wave of pain, he took a huge breath, drew the club high over his head and gave a hoarse roar of victory.

Then all was quiet. Friend unclenched his eyes to see the demon's face as it gnarled into anger, then a question, and finally an expression of confusion as he took note of the tip of a sword, protruding from his chest. It had made its way through the second and third ribs on an upward journey all the way to the monster's heart and beyond. The sword disappeared and the demon fell to the ground with an earth-shattering crash. Now Friend turned his face even more and saw a figure silhouetted against a backdrop of distant lightning. With a supreme effort, Friend was able to focus until he could make out the form of his wife, standing there holding his sword and looking around at the gathered powers and principalities. Her eyes finally rested on the Evil Man, locked into place and waited until all was quiet before she spoke.

"I don't think so."

Think about this

I hope this segment of the story didn't scare you, but I had to make it clear that the enemy of this world is never, nor will he ever be, your advocate. May we never imagine that opposing God will bring favor from Satan's camp. All he wants is your destruction, and he will stop at nothing until he achieves that goal.

But, and here's the good news, Satan will never achieve that goal, neither in this life nor the next. His own destruction is assured just as certainly as is your salvation... provided you accept it. Turn to God today and pray with me: 'Thank you, Lord for Who You are, for what You have done, and for what You will continue to do in my life. Keep me aware of your Presence through both the mountaintops and the valleys.'

Surely goodness and mercy shall follow me all the days of my life, and I shall dwell in the house of the LORD my whole life long.

Psalms 23:6

Episode 14
Confrontation

"I don't think so," Friend's wife announced to the demonic horde surrounding them, staring all the while into the Evil Man's eyes.

He looked down at the slain warrior, then to Friend, who still lay face down in shock and misery, and then at his wife who stood tall, still clutching her husband's sword in her right hand. Taking a step toward her, the Evil Man growled, "What have you done?" Taking another step, he said, "You have no idea what I am capable of. You—"

But then he came to a sudden stop as Friend's wife raised her free left hand, palm toward him. "No. *You* have no idea what *I* am capable of. Actually," she said, lowering her hand and grasping the sword in a two-handed grip, "by myself, I'm capable of nothing. But you know I'm not alone here. I stand before you now in the authority of the One who lives in me: Jesus Christ, Son of the Living God, dwelling in me by His grace and mercy through His Holy Spirit.

"I had a nice chat with Jake... I think you know him? He said that he would love to be here, but that he had more pressing business to attend to. Then he added that his presence is not really needed anyway; there's plenty of firepower here and now to deal with this mob.

"Where to begin? Oh yeah, let's start with your pet poodles. What did Jake call them?" She looked down at her husband. "Chamchas! You've had your fun. Now, by the authority of Jesus Christ, Son of God, come out of him. And don't let me catch you messing with him again, or with me, or with our family. Otherwise, Jake told me about a destination vacation called the Abyss."

That got an immediate response. With shrieks of terror, at least a dozen tiny demons left Friend's body, sailing up over the surrounding hordes and disappearing into the darkness. The effect on Friend was dramatic. Sitting up, he shook his head, rubbed his eyes as he tried to focus, then smiled as he saw his wife standing next to him. "Hey, babe," he said with a rasp in his voice. "Good to see ya. The blade is a nice touch."

At that point, the Evil Man found his voice again. "This is not over. I've summoned my general, who will be arriving soon with his own cohort. Your husband, by the way, actually swore allegiance to him."

"A lie," Friend interrupted. "I *did* allow myself to be cowered by him, retreating when I should have stood my ground. Not the same as 'swearing allegiance'."

"We shall soon see," grinned the Evil Man as he raised his eyes over their heads beyond the demonic principalities looking on in wonder at this encounter. Suddenly, there in a solid ring around and behind them, appeared an army like something out of an apocalyptic vision. Every soldier was decked out with dull black armor, some carrying huge swords, some hoisting long spears, and some with wicked-looking spiked orbs attached to long chains. Each demonic soldier was sitting astride a war horse that never stopped moving, jinking this way and that, eager to join the battle. One horse took a few halting steps forward and stopped. The rider raised his visor to look down on the gathering. Friend recognized him at once as the demonic general he had met at the waterfall.

Gazing over the gathering below, he made eye contact with Friend, then spoke in a voice loud enough for all to hear. "I see that you disobeyed my orders and remained on the mountain. Very well, *pilgrim,* now you shall see just a small sample of the strength I command." Rising up in his stirrups, the general looked around the circle to make sure his soldiers were ready, but when he turned back, there was Jake, standing between Friend and his wife. As before, he stood easily, one arm resting on the handle of a long sword, its point in the ground at his feet. And he was engaged in a conversation with Friend and his wife.

"You know what this reminds me of?" he asked, then answered his own question. "Old Elisha; now *there* was a prophet. Got himself surrounded by his enemies in the town of Dothan. His servant thought they were about to die, until Elisha prayed, 'Oh Lord, please open his eyes that he might see.' And what he saw was not much different from what you're seeing here."

Friend and his wife followed Jake's eyes up, and there, stretching overhead from horizon to horizon stood an army of angelic warriors, too many to count, and every one of them looking to Jake for his signal. As they watched, the scene began to diminish, like a dark cloud was passing overhead. Soon there was nothing visible but black sky in every direction. Jake could see the couple's confusion, and explained. "Some things are not meant to be seen by the Sons of Adam. Not yet at least. There will come a time. For some, sooner than for others," Jake said, with the hint of a smile in Friend's direction. "But for now, just take it on faith that God has not forsaken you. And He never will."

And then Jake was gone, leaving the couple standing alone on the side of the mountain. Where the dark clouds had seemed to envelope everything in their path, stars could now be seen in a sky that was crystal clear. Even as they watched, the stars began to twinkle and disappear, evidence of the coming morning. Looking toward the summit, they could just make out the soft glow of a new day.

Friend's wife helped him to his feet, dusted off the pine needles that covered him, then gave him a big hug. "How do you feel, precious?" she asked, her eyes shut tightly against the tears that demanded release.

Friend kept the embrace going for another minute, then stepped back and took a breath. "Honestly?" he said, "I feel like seeing what's going to happen next."

"Then let's be off," she said, placing his left arm under her shoulder for support.

Think about this:

Why do you think we're not generally allowed to witness events that are going on all around us in the spirit world? Why can't we just see what's happening and erase all doubts as to the reality of our existence? Sorry, but I'm not going to answer that one for you. Think about it. Pray about it. Share it with someone you can trust. Then thank God for His mercy.

When an attendant of the man of God rose early in the morning and went out, an army with horses and chariots was all around the city. His servant said, "Alas, master! What shall we do?" He replied, "Do not be afraid, for there are more with us than there are with them." Then Elisha prayed: "O LORD, please open his eyes that he may see." So the LORD opened the eyes of the servant, and he saw; the mountain was full of horses and chariots of fire all around Elisha.

2 Kings 6:15–17

Episode 15
Near the Summit

The trail led steadily up, toward the top of the mountain, that now stood out in stark contrast against a deep blue sky. The path was not so steep as before, and Friend and his wife were able to walk side by side. With each step, his wounds became less painful and inhibiting, so that instead of keeping his arm over his wife's shoulder for support, he now lowered it to take her hand in his. Watching her out of the corner of his eye, he noticed that she was constantly scanning the area around them, her other hand still maintaining a firm grip on the sword.

"I have to say, babe, I've never seen anyone handle a sword like you did back there. Even in my semi-conscious state, I was impressed."

"Yeah, that kinda surprised me too," she said. "The Rendezvous people showed up at camp not long after you left, and we sat and prayed most of the day. But I never had a chance to talk to anyone about using this thing. I guess it's like what you and I have always taught the new pilgrims: God gives you what you need when you need it."

"You're right, there," Friend said, giving her hand a squeeze. He kept walking a few more steps, then added, "Except…"

"Except what?" she asked, stopping to look at him. She noticed that his face was drawn up in pain, but it was different from the physical hurt that was troubling him before. This went deeper.

"Yesterday," Friend began. "When I met that demon general. It was like nothing I'd ever come up against. I started out a little cocky, I suppose. But before it was over, I was scared; I mean *really* scared. Babe, I needed some courage right then, and well, I got nothing. The next thing I knew, I was lying face down in the mud, tortured by a bunch of troublemakers I should have been able to deal with easily. If you hadn't come along when you did, I hate to think what might have happened."

Leaning the sword against a rock, she took his hands in both of hers and they sat down to rest. They were quiet for a while, then she said, "Let's think about this for a minute. Go back to the last thing you said just now: if I hadn't come back when I did…"

"Exactly!" Friend said. "Just *why* did you come when you did?"

She stood and walked around while she thought. "It started this morning, I guess. I was trying to imagine how I could face the rest of my life without you. Oh, I know the statistics, about nine out of ten married women will spend part of their lives in widowhood. But I just never imagined I'd be one of those nine. We still have our daughter and her husband, and you know the folks at Rendezvous are so much more than family. But just how are things going to work out, and what's my new life going to look like?

"That's when Jake showed up. I was so glad to see him; I had so many questions. Still do, in fact. But he didn't give me a chance to say a word. He just smiled at me and said, *Have I got a job for you.* He explained how you needed my help, and I was being given the chance to do something really important. Of course I was ready and willing. Anything to take my mind off the misery I was feeling. Jake had to stop me and remind me to bring the sword.

"So as far as I was concerned, I received just what I needed when I needed it, as promised. So now the question is, what did *you* need, if not courage to face a big ugly? Is it possible there was something else even more important that needed rescuing, instead of your fear?"

By now, Friend was on his feet, shuffling around as he listened to his wife. Finally, he stopped, looked up toward the summit, looked over at his wife, then went down to his knees, bringing his hands to his face. "Yes... yes... there *was* something more important going on yesterday. I needed something desperately, but it wasn't a shot of courage. In fact, at that moment, the courage to face that demon was the *last* thing I needed.

If I had managed to face him down, then that other, more important need would have remained."

He stood, stepped over to his wife and took her in his arms. "What I needed, more than life itself, was to know that you would be okay after I was gone. Death is not the end of things; you and I both know that. Just as surely as we will see our son again in Heaven, we know that we will see each other as well. *All* of our loved ones will be reunited, every tear will be dried and we'll have all of eternity to celebrate.

"But the thing that makes dying so hard for God's children is the fact that we're leaving behind our loved ones, not knowing how they'll cope... how they'll manage to find a new life and a new reason for living. I know you're a strong woman, babe. I always knew that. But I gotta say, after watching you today, I had no idea just how strong you are! We'll be okay, won't we?"

Think about this:

What is the hardest thing about dying, for a Christian? Death is still a great unknown, of course, and even the strongest faith will falter in the face of one's own mortality. But probably the greatest fear we face is the uncertainty concerning those we leave behind. What will they do? How will they cope? When you pray for the sick, don't forget to pray for those who grieve. May God give strength when strength is needed, and a peace that goes beyond anything the world can give.

Peace I leave with you; my peace I give to you. I do not give to you as the world gives. Do not let your hearts be troubled, and do not let them be afraid.

Episode 16
At the Summit

The trail continued steadily upward through windswept Buffalo grass, growing profusely now that the couple had passed through the timberline beyond which trees could no longer survive. After one final switchback through a boulder field, they broke out onto a large level area about the size of a basketball court. It seemed almost swept clean, and Friend wondered how many others had come to the end of their journey on this spot.

At the far side of the area lay a large stone, made of dark gray granite. Roughly two meters long by one meter wide by a meter high, it could not be mistaken for anything other than what it was: an altar.

"Does it look like it did when you were here... before?" his wife asked.

"Yes. Only beyond the altar was a large staircase, leading upward through the clouds. But that wasn't visible last time either... not at first."

It had been almost a surreal experience. Friend had watched as his son lay on the altar, then rise back up when the blood of a Lamb, flowing down the staircase, had come in contact with him. He would never forget the precious words the Lamb had spoken: "Do not be dismayed. Your son is with me, and in the Father's time, you will also come up these steps. I am the Lamb you sought. I am the way to life."

So now is the 'Father's time', he thought to himself. Then, knowing he may not have another opportunity, he turned to his wife. "We are really blessed to have this chance to say goodbye," he said, holding back tears. "So many others we've known have been taken suddenly and unexpectedly. So… while I have a chance, let me say again how much I've been blessed. As the bride of my youth and the mother of my children, you mean more to me than I could ever express. I know we will meet again, and I pray that until that time, your days will be full of joy and peace. May you accomplish all the work you've been given to do since before you were born. I love you."

She held onto him all the tighter, her own tears soaking the front of his shirt. She said a silent prayer for the ability to speak through her sobs, then looked into his eyes. "How could God have been more wonderful than to lead me to you? I knew from the moment we met that you were special, gifted with a strength that would endure time itself. Even when I could not accept it, when you made the commitment to this journey, still you were strong and patient, never giving up until the Lord finally broke through my rebellious heart. You've given me two precious children, the kind of faithfulness that most women only dream about, and enough adventures to carry me on into however many years I have to wait here." She smiled up at him. "Unlike everyone else on this trail, I know you by the name your mother gave you, but to me you will always be, first and foremost, my precious, precious Friend."

"No better words were ever spoken, by both of you."

They turned to see a Man standing near them. His face was a representation that no artist since the beginning of time had ever successfully captured, but they both knew at once it was Jesus. Immediately they fell together to their knees, but were lifted back up. "No, My Children; not now. At this moment, I want us to be what the Father intended us to be: friends."

They needed no more prompting. They rushed into His arms and basked in the luxury of His embrace. Friend was the first to speak. "I've imagined this moment most of my life. I've been making a list of questions... as I'm sure you know. But right now... I... can't think of a single one."

Jesus gave a soft laugh that seemed to come from the farthest reaches of His heart. "Don't worry, Child, there will be time for you to voice your questions, although you'll find that most of the answers will come to you before then, or else they will lose their significance entirely."

Friend's wife still managed to blurt out, "But, Lord! Why now? And why can't I come? And how will I manage without him?"

Taking His Hands off the couple, He turned to place them both on her shoulders that were shaking uncontrollably. Almost at once, her sobbing ceased and she felt a quietness that she'd never experienced before. "This world is still broken, as you both have been made so painfully aware. My heart is broken as well, to see your grief. But please understand, this is not the world as your Father created it… and it is not the world that is yet to come. Until then, be strong. Remember this moment and share it with others who need it. This is part of the task you've been given: to bring His love to those who have forgotten. When your part is finished, you will join us. I promise."

Looking back at Friend, he said softly, "Now, it is time."

Friend placed his left hand into Jesus' right, and together they turned toward the altar. His wife was not surprised when he did not look back. All had been said, and from this moment on, he was bound for his new home, led by the One Who had prepared it and Who had promised to return for him.

She watched as they approached the altar. They stopped before it, and Jesus said something to Friend that she could not hear. Then they both turned and walked around the altar and toward the staircase that now was plainly visible. They stepped together: once… twice… then they were gone. The staircase disappeared and she was left alone.

But not quite. Jake was there, and when she turned, he placed a hand on her shoulder. "When your son ascended those steps, Friend was distraught. He knew that it was all going to be okay, but first he had to experience a long and painful time of despair. You will not go into that valley, although it will be lonely for you for a long time. For you, there will be a time of cleansing, marked by the kind of grief that all must suffer. But you will be held up by a family the world does not know and could never understand. By their prayers and support each day, you will know peace and joy and the kind of fulfillment that only a Child of God can experience."

Jake pointed down to the path that led into the valley. "There is your way. Walk in it and be blessed."

Think about this:

I realize that putting words into the mouth of God is done only at one's peril. However, I feel certain that what Jesus says in this encounter with Friend and his wife are in keeping with His Word revealed in the Bible. The message for them is the message for you and for me: We live in a broken world that is marked by pain, sickness and suffering, but by God's grace we can know healing and His guiding hand through the difficult times. The love of family is something we will carry on into the Kingdom, but in a form we cannot yet imagine. We are given work to do and the ability to accomplish it. When that work is finished, then in God's time, we will be called to be with Him for eternity. And all of these truths rest on the foundation of faith that we are called to accept: that Jesus Christ, the only begotten Son of God, paid the sacrifice for our sins and by our free acceptance of His gift we become part of His family, promised a place in His Kingdom. Think about these things, then listen for the message He has for you today.

For in him all the fullness of God was pleased to dwell, and through him God was pleased to reconcile to himself all things, whether on earth or in heaven, by making peace through the blood of his cross.

Colossians 1:19–20

Reaching the Heights: Appendix 1
Anger

I hope you've enjoyed this short story, which has now become the third part of my *Road Rising* trilogy. Briefly stated, if you've made it to here, you'll know that the pilgrim known as Friend has come to the end of his journey. With the help of his wife, they have managed to resist the enemy's attempts to make him throw away his faith before he dies. By the way, I purposely avoid attaching names to these characters in the hopes that you, the reader, might identify more easily with them. The story is, after all, about you, and about anyone who faces their own mortality and an uncertain future.

In the story, the couple must come against the deceiving spirits, Denial and Scapegoat, a host of irritating demons called 'chamchas', a brute of a monster that is the stuff of nightmares, a demonic general, and the Evil Man himself. Yes, it's a work of fiction, but the truths portrayed are very real; just ask anyone who has suffered under their persecution.

The idea for the different powers and principalities came from the first book I ever wrote, *Looking for a Lamb*, an allegorical treatment of Christian grief work following the death of our son to leukemia. In that story, a man is taking his son to the top of a mountain where he knows that death awaits. See also the story of Abraham and Isaac. On the way to the summit, the enemy confronts the father with six different temptations to disobey God's command. They come in the form of lambs who can speak (thus the book's title). The seventh and final Lamb of Lambs carries him through to the place where he can accept God's will, whatever that may be.

With your permission, I would like to re-visit those six lambs. Each one represents a stage of grief we all experience at some time in our lives, either grief over past tragedy or that which comes with anticipation of future loss. The first one is often the first that hits us in any attack, and that is the Lamb of Anger.

What makes you angry? Of course there are things such as injustice and irritation that can drive us to the kind of 'holy anger' that the Apostle Paul describes in Ephesians 4:26–27, but the vast majority of the Bible's references to anger are in terms of something to be avoided at all costs. We all know what unbridled anger can do to your health and well-being, and especially to those around us. My son is a policeman, and he nearly shot a man a while back who in his rage was about to make a very foolish decision. Talking about it afterward, my son said, "What a waste it would have been if that man had died because of a moment of uncontrolled anger."

So true, but also so common among us all. Rage accomplishes nothing except to bring pain and suffering. And all too often, its victims are those closest to us.

As Paul wrote, *Be angry but do not sin; do not let the sun go down on your anger, and do not make room for the devil.* How could I say it any better? When you pray today, pray that God would protect you from the anger that boils up from time to time. Pray that He would give you a new perspective and the ability to see that emotion for what it is: the devil's tool sharpened with you in mind.

Reaching the Heights: Appendix 2
The Lamb of Denial

In this, the second of six lambs I want to present to you, we see one of the first responses to shock and grief that we all are likely to experience at one time or another in our lives. That is, we tend to deny the attacks that come our way. I'm not sure this is a fair assessment or not, but I'm told that more men die of prostate cancer than women die of breast cancer, and I can't help but believe that a contributing factor is our tendency to deny there's anything wrong with us until it's too late for effective treatment. In my own defense, I never denied the seriousness of my condition when it was revealed, but was the victim of a particularly sneaky and aggressive version of this 'man disease'.

But all of us, including me, would rather not face harsh realities if they can be avoided, and that's exactly what the enemy of this world uses to his advantage. He'll be the first to smile and agree with your hesitation. "Of *course* you don't want to face something so unthinkable! And why should you? You feel fine, right? Just turn back."

This 'she'll be right, mate' way of thinking has gotten we Aussies through many a difficult situation, and truth be known, has steered us away from a lot of unnecessary stress and worry. As Christians, even, we know that at the end of the day, she *will* be right, in terms of God's ultimate victory over a sin-battered world. But there are times when in spite of the Bible's assurances about all things evil, we are called to confront them rather than deny their existence.

And the reason is fairly simple: God created us to be fighters. When sin entered into the world, two of the first curses involved sweat-of-your-brow hard yakka when it comes to making a living, and you-gotta-be-kidding pain when it comes to childbirth (Genesis 3:16–19). And no one today would doubt the reality of those first two results of sin in the world. But listen: God said, "You have to face it," but He didn't say, "You have to take it." I'm not sure how Eve dealt with the childbearing challenge, but I suspect Adam made himself a sharper stick with which to till the ground, and if he had had access to a John Deere tractor, I'm sure he would have learned how to use it. This is not rebellion against God's decrees but rather using the strengths He gave us to overcome the challenges of living in a broken world.

And if I need any reminders of this truth, I need look no farther than the next chapter of Genesis I just quoted above. You know the story: Cain and Abel. Younger brother's attempts to please God are accepted, but Cain's were not. His first response was the one I reported about last week as he buckled under the temptations from the Lamb of Anger. But listen to God's words as he warns the young man:

The LORD said to Cain, "Why are you angry, and why has your countenance fallen? If you do well, will you not be accepted? And if you do not do well, sin is lurking at the door; its desire is for you, but you must master it." (Genesis 4:6–7)

Did you catch that? The enemy 'desires' to eat your lunch, but in the Words of God Himself, 'you must master it'. So when bad things come your way, be it a nagging headache, a field of weeds that needs clearing or a doctor's diagnosis, pray about it first to see if God has any special instructions in this instance, then throw off the gloves and fight. Take an aspirin for the pain, get a bigger tool for the job, listen to your doctor and do what he says. What you *don't* want to do is think, 'Well, this is my lot in life; I'm a Christian so I'll have to accept it'.

It's attitudes like that, that have given Christianity its milk toast image. I'll say again, and leave you with it: when troubles come your way, don't give in to temptation's insistence that you can simply deny them and go on about your life. Look to God for a reality check, then look to the things that challenge you. Use the gifts, the strengths, the abilities you've been given and be a warrior.

Reaching the Heights: Appendix Three
The Warrior Lamb

In Appendix Two, I encouraged you to throw off your denial and be a warrior. Now I need to temper that with these words: 'Pick your battles, and 'Pick your side'.

Instead of the Warrior Lamb you may have met in my book, *Looking for a Lamb*, in this short story, I've shown you a more realistic and terrifying picture in the form of the demon general. In describing him, I was thinking of those four horsemen of the Apocalypse, found in Revelation 9:13 and following. These are the true stuff of nightmares, locked away in a place known as the Abyss until the time has come for their deadly work. One day during the Tribulation, they will be released, and before they finish, they and the two-hundred-million-strong army they command will kill one third of mankind.

The demon general in this story tried to convince Friend to deny his faith and join those in rebellion against God. And he strengthened his argument by reminding the pilgrim that, wherever you go in the world, Christians are in a sad minority. Is it possible that we are, in fact, on the losing side? When the battle lines are finally drawn up at Armageddon, will our Lord make short work of the demon army as His Word says He will? Or, will things play out altogether differently?

My father was in the Navy during World War II, and he sometimes spoke in low tones about the fear he and his loved ones experienced in those uncertain times. "The fact is," he told me, "we didn't know *how* it was going to end. We had to come to grips with the possibility that we just might lose this conflict." And the history books would agree with him. There were pivotal moments in both the Pacific and the European theaters that turned the tide of war, but those moments could have gone either way.

Fortunately, for those who by faith follow our Creator, we know Armageddon's outcome. God's victory is assured. The enemy will be vanquished and all those who follow him will be cast into the lake of fire. If you don't have that assurance today, I urge you to make this your number one priority. Pick your battles. Pick your side. Today, while you still have the choice. It's the most important decision you will ever make.

Reaching the Heights: Appendix Four
The Lamb of Trade

We didn't meet the Lamb of Trade in this story, and that was because the pilgrim had already dealt successfully with him on his first journey up the mountain, with his son. The lie had been laid out simply: "For everything, there is a price, including the life of your son. As the Lamb of Trade, I will pay that price, and you will be in my debt."

On one level, the offer makes sense. This is, after all, the way things work in the Western World. Capitalism at its finest. As products of that mindset, we are quick to establish a value on anything and everything within our reach. By our way of thinking, it's not a question of whether or not something is available, but rather, how much must I pay? And when it comes to the life of a loved one, there is no price too dear.

Enter the Lamb of Trade.

If we are to be those *wise and innocent sheep* in the midst of wolves (Matthew 10:16), then we must be quick to see the lie. In the first place, the Lamb of Trade is incapable of providing the service he offers. He has no authority over life and death, and whatever he holds up is not what he promises. In the second place, even if there was a debt, rest assured that it has been paid already. Jesus Christ, on the Cross, covered the cost and declared us free of obligation. The only requirement remaining is to accept the gift.

Problems come when we fail to recognize the extent of what we received. We still live in a broken world, surrounded by the suffering and sickness that comes with sin's horrific consequences. But when Jesus promises life in all its abundance (John 10:10), he's not limiting that to the daily hurts that come our way. At times, in His Sovereignty, He will intercede even in these things and grant healing, peace and comfort. But the gift of life that is ours is a gift that goes beyond this fleeting time; we are given instead a life without end, sharing the joys of God's people in God's Kingdom. From that standpoint, we will someday look back on this life and be amazed at how short and trivial it appears next to eternity. But for today, we must look with suspicion at the Lamb of Trade. See him for who he really is, and what he really claims to be offering.

Then show him the receipt that was given you by God's own Son, and dismiss him with great prejudice.

Reaching the Heights: Appendix Five
The Scapegoat

Is anyone *not* familiar with the term, 'scapegoat'? Historically, of course, the concept comes from the Old Testament, specifically, the sixteenth chapter of Leviticus. There, the children of Israel were instructed to take two goats, draw straws, and send one into the wilderness as a powerful symbol of one who takes away the sins of the people. This became an important part of Israel's annual Yom Kippur, a fitting foundation for the coming of Jesus, Who would be the *Lamb of God, Who takes away the sin of the world* (John 1:29).

The pilgrim in the story you just read, on his first ascent of the mountain with his son (from the book, *Looking for a Lamb)*, was confronted by a lamb known as Scapegoat. Incredibly, he offered to go to the summit and there pay for the life of the pilgrim's son with his own. It soon became obvious that he had no intention of carrying out that promise, but was trying to get the poor man to turn around and go back down with his son, rather than move forward in obedience.

As one of the Big Six I want to introduce here, Scapegoat is a regular visitor to anyone dealing with grief. Remember that the enemy's goal, at the end of the day, is to get you to turn back on your promises to God, throw away your faith and take your chances with whatever the world has to offer. One doesn't have to look far to see the process at work; it just seems to come naturally.

Our kids were great examples of the Scapegoat principle. We would turn away from the dinner table and look back to see milk spilled all over. The guilty party would look at the ceiling, then say something like, "Um, the milk got spilled." This implied of course that the culprit was anyone but the child under the spotlight.

As parents, we felt it was important to establish responsibility at an early age, and so we would respond with, "Can you say, *I* spilled the milk?" That was met with varying degrees of success, but I hope the kids got the message early on that it's always important to place the blame where blame is due. Why is it important? Because we've seen so many broken families where Scapegoat has had his way.

When bad times come, the temptation is quick to appear, and fairly predictable. The focus of our blame is usually directed at:

1. The first person in reach,
2. God, or,
3. Self.

Blaming any one of these targets has the power to destroy a person and take away any possibility for resolution and forgiveness. Some short examples from my own experience as a pastor:

A man blames his wife for his own weakness because, "She should have known about it, and helped me when I needed it."

A mother and father blamed God for the death of their daughter, believing that, "God needed another angel, so He took our precious child."

A young man, feeling helpless about his drug addiction, takes his own life, telling his loved ones that, "It's all my fault; I'm to blame and I have to pay."

Take note of these examples. I'm not commenting on the legitimacy of the blame that was placed; only on the outcomes: broken family, bitter parents and tragic death.

God has a better way.

Scapegoat's temptation is based on an element of truth: something is wrong and must be made right. As humans, we are easy targets for this attack. We agree, after all, with the need for retribution. Scapegoat strokes that understanding, and reminds us that *we* must suffer. It's at precisely that point that the Better Way comes in. Retribution has already happened, through the Blood of Jesus Christ. There is no need to listen to Scapegoat's offer to be a substitute. To do so would be, at best, a waste of time, at worst, a broad pathway to sin.

Reaching the Heights: Appendix Six
The Magician's Lamb

Who doesn't believe in magic? Think about it before you answer. Just what *is* 'magic', by your definition? At the end of the day, we're hard-wired to all things logical. That definition may differ from culture to culture, but we all have a box set of expectations, within which we feel 'normal'. Anything outside that box demands an explanation, and when it can't be found, we're faced with the possibility that what we're seeing is somehow *supernatural*; dare we say, *magic*?

Magic provides an easy out for difficult and convoluted movie and book plots. Does the story seem impossible to resolve? Simple. Add a touch of magic, and everything works out beautifully.

The offer of magic also comes to us in times of great personal need. Are you or someone you love facing an incurable sickness or an impossible problem? Enter the Enemy with a too-good-to-be-true solution: magic.

The Magician's Lamb appeared to the pilgrim in *Looking for a Lamb* with a mysterious object he called a 'token'. The temptation was simple: pick up the token and your son will live. How that would come about was not explained, which is, after all, the essence of magic, isn't it? Mere mortals are not *meant* to know the mysteries behind the veil; we are simply told to complete a quest, and we will be magically rewarded. Come to think of it, I'm told that when Marsha was in fourth grade, she would promise to love any boy who could carry a huge rock around the playground. Then again, I don't think that's so much magic as emerging hormones. I wonder how many men today walk with a permanent limp because of her 'quest challenge'?

The Magician's Lamb is never far away, especially when we find ourselves with difficult, seemingly impossible situations. His solutions may sound implausible, but those are the very times when in our desperation we are prepared to consider anything. But consider we must. Just what is the price of the mystery? Remember that the Enemy's promise of God-like power only required that we eat from a particular tree. And the option was necessary, after all; otherwise, obedience without the option to disobey is nothing less than slavery. God could just as easily have placed a park bench in the Garden with a sign that said, 'Don't sit here'. By choosing to sit or not, we demonstrate our willingness to submit to God's authority… or not.

Let me end this discussion with a quote from *Looking for a Lamb:* 'Those who do good in the name of the one whose name is Evil, those who use the spiritual truths of the heavenly realm and twist them into praise for the Destroyer himself: they must be challenged. The ground they stand on must be shown as the quicksand it is. We ourselves must hold the high ground, firmly established on the Rock whose Name is the only one that brings true healing. The Magician's Lamb is a shrewd adversary. Fear him. Fight him. Flee from him."

Reaching the Heights: Appendix Seven
The Demon Lamb

I can count on the fingers of one hand the times in my life when I could sense a demonic presence nearby. Sharing one of those encounters with a Christian friend whose opinion I trusted, he listened quietly till I was finished, then broke into a smile. "Rejoice!" he said, "The Enemy has gotten so desperate he had to show himself!"

Thinking about that over the years, I have to agree. Satan and his minions would rather do their work in darkness, knowing that our imaginations can be so much more effective than reality. And the reality is, demons are nothing more than defeated things, stripped of their authority and left with no greater weapon than their powers of deception.

That was the case for the pilgrim in *Looking for a Lamb*. The demon appeared only as two large eyes in total darkness towering over the poor man. It was only when God's Light shone, the creature was revealed as something like a small possum with extra-large eyes.

Remember the passage from Genesis 4:6–7 I quoted back in Appendix Two? God warned Cain to be on the lookout for the enemy who wanted to devour him. *It desires to have you, but you must master it.* Cain heard this, but he didn't listen; and keep this in mind: *Satan* did not kill Abel. Cain did it himself, believing it would accomplish something to his advantage.

The last time I sensed a demonic presence nearby, was just after my son had died of leukemia. I was walking in the dark, like the pilgrim in *Looking for a Lamb*. And while I didn't see two eyes staring down at me, I could imagine them as clearly as I imagine this keyboard in front of me. And while I didn't hear an audible voice, I got the message loud and clear, and it went straight to my heart. "*I* killed your son," he said, "because you were involved in things that were not your concern. Now, *back off,* or who in your family might be next?"

I confess that I was terrified. I told Marsha, "If he can make good on that threat, I'm going to have to think long and hard before I open my mouth again." It took a lot of prayer and a lot of prayer warriors around me for three days before I had that 'Aha!' moment. *Wait a minute!* I thought. *Satan in a liar. He has no authority over my life or anyone else's. He can scare me, if I'm not prepared, but he can't touch me, and that's a promise.*

I hope you never experience a demonic encounter, but if you do, rejoice! Satan has failed in his more subtle ways with you, and has had to reveal himself. When that happens, you've got him right where you want him. Remember, if you're a child of God, he can't hurt you.

Remind him of that fact, and refer all future communications to your Father.

You believe there is one God. Good! Even the demons believe that — and shudder.

James 2:19

Reaching the Heights: Appendix Eight
The Lamb of Lambs

Over a fifty-year career, I have served as an ambulance attendant in Colorado and California, missionary in three third-world and four first-world countries, and as pastor in more churches than I could count. As a result, I have stood in close proximately to many people who found themselves at death's doorway. And yet, I'm afraid, that only makes me all the less qualified to write about what to expect when one's final breath is drawn. I have attempted here in *Reaching the Heights* to do just that, but I have to realize that those experiences will in no way prepare you for the day when you come face-to-face with your Maker.

On the other hand, I believe I can say in all confidence that the final words of the previous sentence are true and accurate: every man, woman and child will one day find himself or herself before the Creator of all things. Whether that meeting is an occasion for sublime joy or sheer terror depends in large part on the relationship between the two of you before the final day comes. In the case of the pilgrim whose name was Friend, and his wife whose name was never revealed, my faith tells me that the meeting will be one of pure bliss, in spite of the reality of husband and wife coming to a time of parting. I have this assurance because I hold God's Word as found in the Bible to be true and trustworthy, and it is because of that very thing that this book has been written, and for that matter every other book my wife and I have produced over a lifetime.

Our lives will always come complete with a variety of lambs, each one trying in his own way to convince us to turn back from the journey, deny the faith that lifts us and give nodding assent to our adversary. We need not be surprised when these challenges come our way, but we might be forgiven for our reaction to the ways in which they come. The enemy of this world has been in the business of deception for a long, long time, and he often knows just how to present his case. But we can take comfort in the fact that God knows him perfectly, just as He knows you and me, and so we can read in confidence the worlds of the Apostle Paul in 1st Corinthians 10:13, *No testing has overtaken you that is not common to everyone. God is faithful, and he will not let you be tested beyond your strength, but with the testing he will also provide the way out so that you may be able to endure it.*

Allow me to leave you with this promise: as I transfer these thoughts to words, and as the words find their way to form, either by printer's ink or by digital impulses, I am praying for you, the Reader. I am convinced that it was not by chance that you find yourself at this moment considering the Lamb of Lambs and His role in your life. May His grace and mercy find their way into your heart. May your heart be pliable in His loving Hands, and may you continue to become all that He has created you to be: a faithful pilgrim on a journey to the heights He has set before you. At the end of the journey, may your meeting with Him be a time of pure joy, and a time of hearing those precious Words, *Well done, good and faithful servant. You have been faithful in a few things, now I will put you in charge of many things. Enter into the joy of your Master.* (Matthew 25:21)

Travel well.

www.ingramcontent.com/pod-product-compliance
Lightning Source LLC
LaVergne TN
LVHW091558060526
838200LV00036B/892